## GOOSE ON THE LOOSE

'Mr Hadcroft made a mistake and brought the wrong goose,' said James. 'You got little Penny Hapwell's pet goose. So if you give us Gussie back, we'll get you another one.'

Mr Barber looked at them. 'And what would I want to do that for?' he said. 'I've got a goose.'

'But that goose is Penny's pet,' said Mandy.

Mr Barber leaned towards them. 'I told the vicar and I'll tell you and anybody else that asks,' he said. 'I won that goose fair and square in the raffle. It's mine and nobody else's.'

Mandy sighed and turned towards the door. 'Why don't you like animals, Mr Barber?' she asked.

Mr Barber looked up. 'Who said I didn't?' he asked. 'I like geese – to eat! And I intend to eat my goose for lunch this Sunday – with all the trimmings!'

*Animal Ark series*

# LUCY DANIELS
# Goose
## *—on the—*
# Loose

*Illustrations by Shelagh McNicholas*

**Hodder
Children's
Books**

a division of Hodder Headline plc

**Special thanks to Helen Magee**
**Thanks also to C. J. Hall, B.Vet.Med., M.R.C.V.S., for reviewing**
**the veterinary information contained in this book.**

Text copyright © 1996 Ben M. Baglio
Created by Ben M. Baglio
London W6 0HE

Illustrations copyright © Shelagh McNicholas 1996

First published in Great Britain in 1996
by Hodder Children's Books

The right of Lucy Daniels to be identified as the Author of
this Work has been asserted by her in accordance with the
Copyright, Designs and Patents Act 1988.

20  19  18  17  16  15  14  13

A Catalogue record for this book is available from the British Library

ISBN 0 340 64087 1

Typeset by Avon Dataset Ltd, Bidford-on-Avon B50 4JH

Printed and bound in Great Britain by
Clays Ltd, St Ives plc

Hodder Children's Books
a division of Hodder Headline plc
338 Euston Road
London NW1 3BH

For Laura Shaw,
a fan of *Animal Ark* – and a very careful reader!

# *One*

'I'm really looking forward to seeing Cally again,' Mandy Hope said. She leaned over her dad's shoulder and looked out of the windscreen of the Land-rover as they passed Welford Village Hall.

Mr Hope glanced at her briefly and smiled. 'And what about Penny?' he said as he drove past the Fox and Goose pub and up towards the moors.

Mandy laughed. 'I'm looking forward to seeing Penny too,' she said.

'But cats are more interesting,' James Hunter said, pushing his glasses up his nose. James's glasses were always sliding down his nose.

'Too right, James,' said Mr Hope.

Mandy grinned and shook her blonde hair back from her face. Both her parents were vets in Welford, a small village in Yorkshire. They were always teasing her about liking animals more than people.

'Poor Cally,' she said. 'It was such a nasty accident.' Mandy's blue eyes clouded. She was thinking of the time when Cally had cut her leg badly on some farm machinery. The poor little animal had almost died.

'Cally's fine now,' Mr Hope said. 'It's Titan, his prize bull, that Tom Hapwell is worried about.'

Mandy's face was concerned. Titan was an enormous black bull. Tom Hapwell had called him Titan because of his size.

'But Titan is so strong,' she said. 'Surely there can't be anything seriously wrong with him.'

Mr Hope shook his head. 'I won't know until I've seen him, but it sounds like a skin complaint. It could be ringworm.'

'What's that?' said Mandy.

'It's a skin disease caused by fungi,' said Mr Hope. 'And it can be very difficult to get rid of. In fact, once an animal has had it, it's likely to come back. It's also very contagious.'

'You mean the other cattle could get it?' Mandy said.

Mr Hope nodded. 'And not just the cattle. People can catch it too,' he said. 'It's a nasty thing.'

'You'll cure it, Mr Hope,' James said. 'Just like you cured Cally when she was a kitten.'

Mandy smiled. James was her best friend. He was a year younger than she was. He lived in Welford too and he and Mandy cycled to school in Walton together every day. James liked animals nearly as much as Mandy did.

'I certainly hope so, James,' Mr Hope said. 'That bull of Tom Hapwell's is worth a lot of money.'

Mr Hope slowed the Land-rover to negotiate a bend in the road. Then they began the climb up Twyford Hill. Mandy looked at her father. He had dark hair and a beard and the kind of lopsided smile that makes you want to smile too.

'You'd cure it even if it wasn't worth a lot of money, Dad,' Mandy said.

'You're right, I would,' said Mr Hope. 'But the bull was a big investment for Tom Hapwell. Farmers don't keep animals as pets, you know. They have to earn their keep.'

'Penny has a pet goose as well as a young cat,' said James.

Mr Hope chuckled. 'Gussie,' he said. 'That goose is nearly as much trouble as Blackie.'

'Dad!' said Mandy, outraged. She turned to James.

But James was laughing. 'You must admit, Mandy,' he said. 'Blackie isn't the most obedient dog in the world.'

Blackie was James's pet Labrador.

'No, but he's the nicest one,' Mandy said.

'So he is,' said Mr Hope. 'Only joking, James.'

'I know that,' said James. He looked at Mandy. 'And so does Mandy,' he said.

Mandy was very proud of her dad – and of her mum too. Emily and Adam had adopted Mandy when her own parents were killed in a car crash. Mandy had been only a baby at the time. She couldn't even remember her natural parents. But that never troubled her. As far as she was concerned she had the best parents in the world in Adam and Emily Hope.

'Isn't it beautiful up here?' said Mandy.

She looked out of the Land-rover window. They were up on the moors above Welford now. Mandy could see the village nestling in the valley – the Fox and Goose where Mr Hardy was landlord, the post office that Mr and Mrs McFarlane ran, Lilac Cottage, where Gran and Grandad lived, and best of all Animal Ark, the Hopes' surgery and their home.

'It's hard on the farmers up here in winter,' said Mr Hope. 'But on a lovely spring evening like this it's . . .' He stopped.

'Heaven,' said Mandy.

'Heaven,' Mr Hope agreed, laughing.

'There's the track,' James said, pointing out of the window.

Mr Hope changed down a gear and turned on to the farm track to Twyford.

The Land-rover rattled over the cattle grid and into the farmyard. A little girl with a mop of curly dark hair came running out of the farmhouse. She was dressed in blue dungarees and bright yellow gumboots. Her face lit up as she saw who it was.

'Mandy! James!' she called. 'Come and see Cally!'

Mandy waved at little Penny Hapwell as Mr Hope stopped in front of the cattle shed. Then she opened the door and jumped down.

'Hi, Penny,' she said.

A man in old corduroy trousers and a checked shirt strode out of the cattle shed. It was Tom Hapwell, Penny's dad.

'Penny's been watching for you,' he said to Mandy. He smiled at Penny. 'She's got Cally all dressed up for you,' he said.

Mandy grinned. 'Oh, I'm looking forward

seeing Cally,' she replied. 'She must have grown since the last time I saw her.'

''Morning, Tom,' said Mr Hope. 'What's the problem with Titan?'

Tom Hapwell shook his head. 'It beats me,' he said. 'There's a sore patch on his flank and it seems to be getting bigger. He's starting to rub it on anything he can get near so it must be bothering him.'

Mandy watched her dad and Tom Hapwell disappear into the cattle shed. Penny tugged at her hand.

'Come *on*!' she said urgently.

Mandy laughed and let herself be dragged into the farmhouse kitchen. Although Penny was a lot smaller than them, she was very determined.

Mrs Hapwell was baking. 'Mmm,' said James. 'Something smells good.'

'Hello, Mandy. Hi, James,' Mrs Hapwell said. Then she saw the look on James's face. 'Five minutes and the scones will be ready,' she said. 'But first you've got to admire Cally.'

Penny ran to a basket beside the kitchen stove and scooped up a furry bundle.

'Here she is,' the little girl said, thrusting the tortoiseshell kitten at Mandy. There was a red ribbon tied to her collar.

Mandy took Cally gently and laughed. Cally looked up at her and batted a paw, trying to reach the ribbon. 'She *is* dressed up, isn't she?' Mandy said.

Penny nodded. 'Specially for you,' she said.

Mandy tweaked the red ribbon that was tied round Cally's collar. Cally didn't look too pleased about the ribbon. 'And don't you look gorgeous?' she said to the young cat. She held Cally up in front of her and gazed into the big green eyes.

Cally blinked and gave a little miaow.

'She really *is* well again,' Mandy said.

Mrs Hapwell nodded. 'As good as new,' she said. Mandy felt a lump rise in her throat. She remembered the day Mrs Hapwell and Penny had brought Cally into the surgery. The kitten had been covered in blood from her injuries, hardly able to move. And now she was trying to struggle out of Mandy's grasp.

'OK,' said Mandy. 'Let's see you run,' she said and she set the kitten down on the floor.

Cally stretched and arched her back, then she scampered off and began to tug at the laces on James' shoes.

'You made her better,' Penny said, looking at Mandy.

Mandy shook her head. 'Not me,' she said. 'Mum

and Dad are the vets. They make the animals better.'

'But you looked after her,' Penny insisted.

Mandy looked at Mrs Hapwell.

'You can't deny it, Mandy,' Mrs Hapwell said. 'You know you would look after any animal. And you're a great help to your mum and dad.'

Mandy blushed. But she didn't get a chance to reply. Mrs Hapwell turned to take the freshly baked scones out of the oven. She scooped half a dozen on to a plate, split them and spread butter on them.

'Help yourself,' she said, smiling at Mandy and James. 'I'm just going to take these out to Tom and your dad.' And she bustled out of the door into the farmyard.

James picked up a scone and took a bite. 'Mmm,' he said. 'These are fantastic.'

Mandy turned back and found Penny's eyes on her. The little girl bit her lip. Then she took a deep breath.

'Any animal?' she said.

Mandy's brow furrowed. 'What?' she said.

'Mummy said you would look after any animal,' Penny said. 'Would you?'

Mandy thought for a moment. She tried very hard to think of an animal she wouldn't want to look after.

She couldn't think of a single one.

'Yes,' she said. 'I suppose I would.'

Penny swallowed hard and her face screwed up with excitement. 'Even Gussie?' she said.

'Gussie?' said Mandy, puzzled.

Penny nodded. 'Gussie,' she repeated. 'My goose.'

Mandy laughed. 'I know who Gussie is,' she said. 'You looked after her when she was a baby, didn't you?'

Penny nodded. 'Daddy has lots of geese. But Gussie is all mine,' she said. 'She wasn't very well when she was born and the other geese were bad to her.' Penny's mouth turned down. 'They pecked her,' she said.

Mandy nodded sympathetically. 'That happens sometimes,' she said.

'So Mummy and I looked after her,' said Penny. 'And now she's mine.'

'Your very own pet goose,' said Mandy. 'That's lovely, Penny.'

'But now Mummy and I are going to stay with Granny for a weekend and Mummy says I can take Cally.'

'That'll be nice,' said Mandy.

'But I can't take Gussie,' said Penny. 'Because Granny lives in a flat in the town.'

'That wouldn't be very good for a goose,' Mandy said gently.

Penny nodded. 'I know,' she said. 'But if I leave Gussie here she might get out of her pen. Sometimes she does, you know. She's very clever. And she'll be lonely without me. She's used to having me looking after her all the time. What if she gets out of her pen and comes looking for me? What if she gets in beside the other geese? They might peck her again.' She lifted her eyes to Mandy.

Mandy looked at Penny. The little girl's eyes were filled with tears. It was no good trying to reassure her. She would worry the whole weekend about Gussie.

'I don't want Gussie to get pecked again,' she said. 'So, if you really would look after *any* animal, would you look after Gussie for me?'

Mandy swallowed. She looked at James.

'Get out of that,' he said, shaking his floppy brown hair out of his eyes.

Mandy shook her head. She should have seen it coming. But a goose! What on earth was she going to do with a goose for a weekend? It was all very well if you lived on a farm. Geese belonged on a farm.

'That might be difficult, Penny,' she began. Then she stopped.

Penny's tears had overflowed and her cheeks were wet. The little girl put up a hand and wiped a tear away.

'But you *said* you would look after *any* animal,' she said. 'And Daddy is too busy to bother with Gussie. And if she goes in with the other geese she might get *pecked*.'

Mandy took a deep breath. Penny was right. If a pet goose was put in with the other farm geese, the other geese might well go for it. And if that happened, Mandy would feel awful.

Mandy took a deep breath. 'Don't you worry, Penny,' she said. 'Of course I'll look after Gussie for you.'

Penny's tears dried like magic and her face broke into a smile. 'Really?' she said. 'Really and truly?'

'Really and truly,' said Mandy.

Penny let out an enormous sigh of relief. 'And now I won't have to worry about Gussie,' she said. 'I know she'll be safe with you, Mandy!'

Mandy smiled back but her mind was whirling. It was true that Mandy couldn't resist any animal – especially one that was in danger of being harmed. But her mum was very strict about taking animals into Animal Ark. She had told Mandy often that Animal Ark was for sick animals. Mandy sighed to herself. Mrs Hope was right. If Mandy had her way, Animal Ark would be overrun with pets. But her problem remained. What was she going to do with Gussie? She couldn't get out of it. She had promised.

'Come on,' Penny was saying. 'I'll show you where Gussie lives. Daddy made a special pen just for her.'

Penny skipped out of the door and Mandy and James followed.

'You walked right into that,' said James.

Mandy looked at him helplessly. 'What else could I do?' she said.

James grinned. 'It isn't what you've done, it's what you've still *got* to do that's the problem,' he said.

'What's that?' said Mandy

James's grin got even wider. 'Persuade your mum that having Gussie the goose as a weekend guest is a good idea,' he said.

Mandy groaned. Why could she never say no to an animal in trouble?

# Two

'Maybe I could wriggle out of it somehow,' Mandy said as she and James followed Penny round the side of the farmhouse.

'And disappoint Penny?' James said.

Mandy sighed. Then her face lit up as they came in sight of the goose pen. 'Oh, look!' she said. 'Isn't she lovely?' She ran towards the pen where a long-necked goose was looking curiously at them.

Gussie's feathers were creamy white, except for one wing which was dark grey. It gave Gussie a slightly lopsided look. Her bill and legs were bright orange and her broad webbed feet looked very strong.

Penny opened the door of the pen and beckoned to Mandy. 'Gussie wants to meet you,' she said.

Mandy walked into the pen and stood about a metre away from Gussie. Geese could be very tame if reared from young but even pet geese could snap sometimes. Gussie looked at her with bright black eyes, sizing her up.

'Don't come too near at first, James,' she said. 'Geese have very strong necks and bills.'

'Gussie won't hurt you,' Penny said.

'We don't want to frighten her,' Mandy said.

James and Mandy stood quietly while Gussie had a good look at them. The goose lowered her head, spread her wings a little and hissed warningly.

'She always does that with strangers,' Penny said. 'You know, geese make very good watchdogs. But she's really friendly once you get to know her.'

Penny marched up to her pet goose and tapped her on her bright orange bill.

'Now, now, Gussie,' the little girl said. 'You've got to be friends with Mandy and James. Mandy is going to look after you while I'm away.'

Gussie turned a bright black eye on Penny and folded her wings. Then she waddled over and stood in front of Mandy. She stretched her neck up and honked.

Mandy laughed and stretched out a hand. The goose's feathers felt incredibly soft under her fingertips. Gussie honked again and snuggled close to Mandy's legs, almost as if she was asking for affection.

'There,' said Penny in a satisfied voice. 'I told you Gussie would like you.'

Mandy and James looked at each other.

'Looks like we've just acquired a goose for the weekend,' Mandy said to James.

'You'll do it? You'll look after Gussie for me?' Penny said.

Mandy nodded and Penny bent down and slid an

arm round Gussie's neck. 'There, Gussie,' she said. 'What did I tell you? You won't be lonely after all. Mandy and James are going to look after you!'

'But I promised,' Mandy said to her dad for the umpteenth time. 'And it's only for the weekend.'

They had dropped James off on the way home.

Mr Hope shook his head. 'Try telling that to your mum,' he said. 'And she's quite right. If you had your way we would be living in a zoo.'

Mandy grinned in spite of her worries and Mr Hope ruffled her hair.

'Cheer up,' he said. 'Your mum is very fond of little Penny. She wouldn't want to see her worried about Gussie being pecked – or being lonely.'

Mandy bit her lip. Adam Hope was more easy going than his wife. Mrs Hope was the business person in their house. It wasn't that she was unkind. Far from it. She was the kindest person in the world. But she was practical and she realised they couldn't take in every waif and stray that came their way. Somebody had to be practical, Mandy thought ruefully. But why did it have to be Mrs Hope?

'We're home,' said Mr Hope.

Mandy looked up. Animal Ark came into view and Mandy couldn't help smiling. She loved it so much.

The wooden sign that said 'Animal Ark, Veterinary Surgeon' swung in the breeze. Banks of flowers bordered the path leading up to the old stone cottage. It had a modern extension at the back where the surgery was.

As Mandy watched, two figures came round the corner of the house and stopped. 'There's Mum,' she said. 'And Gran.'

Mrs Hope's curly red hair was tied back with a green scarf and her white lab coat gleamed in the early evening sunlight. She smiled and waved as the Land-rover came to a halt.

'Hi, Mum! Hi, Gran!' Mandy called, racing over to them.

'And all I can say is the sooner the McFarlanes are back the better!' Gran was saying as Mandy drew up.

'The McFarlanes? Where have they gone?' said Mandy.

Gran turned to her. 'To Scotland,' Gran said. 'Their daughter has just had a baby and they've gone up there to give her a hand for a couple of weeks.'

'Does that mean the post office is closed?' said Mandy. 'What are we going to do without it?'

Gran had organised a vigorous campaign to keep the post office open when it was threatened with closure. After all, it was the heart of the village. You didn't just get stamps and newspapers and comics there. You got all the local gossip as well – from Mrs McFarlane. If anything was going on in Welford or even in Walton, the nearest town, Mrs McFarlane always knew about it first.

Gran shook her head. 'It isn't closed,' she said. 'But they've got a temporary postmaster over from Walton. He's living in the little flat above the post office and to hear him you'd think he owned the place.'

'Why? What's he done?' said Mandy.

'Only upset half the village already,' said Gran. 'And he's only been here two days. Mrs Ponsonby says she'll never set foot in the post office again – or at least not till the McFarlanes are back.'

Mrs Ponsonby was a large, bossy woman who lived at Bleakfell Hall, one of the biggest houses in Welford. She told everybody what to do – and expected them to do it! But she had taken in Toby, a stray puppy nobody else wanted, so she wasn't all bad. Mandy would always be grateful to Mrs Ponsonby for that, even though she tried to keep out of her way if she could.

'What did he do to her?' Mandy asked, her eyes round.

Gran pursed her lips. 'He made her rewrap a parcel three times before he would accept it. He said it didn't fit the regulations the way she had wrapped it.'

Mandy bit her lip to stop herself grinning. She could just imagine how Mrs Ponsonby would react to being bossed about for a change!

'And he made Walter Pickard sign his pension book again in front of him,' Gran said indignantly. 'He wouldn't believe it was Walter's signature unless he saw him do it.' Gran tossed her head. 'Talk about pernickety,' she said. 'As if Walter would trick anybody!'

Walter Pickard was a retired butcher. He lived in a cottage behind the Fox and Goose with his three cats and was a bell-ringer at the church with Grandad. He was as honest as the day was long.

'That must have upset Walter,' Mandy said.

Gran nodded. 'And Mr High and Mighty Temporary Postmaster was annoyed with me for putting a stamp on a letter upside down. I'd forgotten my reading glasses. It looked all right to me.' Gran looked at her watch. 'I must get back,' she said. 'I've got some packing to do.'

'Are you going away?' Mandy asked.

Gran and Grandad had a camper-van, like a

miniature house on wheels. There had been no holding them since they'd got it. Now that Grandad was retired, they could take off any time they wanted to and they were always going on trips in it. Mr Hope said they were turning into real globe-trotters.

Gran nodded. 'We thought we'd go off on Saturday. Just for a couple of days,' she said. 'We'll be back on Monday.' She gave Mandy a kiss. 'I'll bring you a present.'

'Where from?' Mandy said.

Gran's eyes twinkled. 'Who knows?' she said. 'Grandad and I have decided just to go where the mood takes us.'

Mandy grinned. Globe-trotters – just like Dad said.

''Bye, Gran,' she said as her grandmother walked down the path towards the Land-rover.

Gran turned, rummaging in her bag. 'Did I give you your raffle tickets?' she said to Emily Hope.

Mrs Hope put a hand in her lab coat pocket and pulled out a sheaf of bright pink tickets. 'Two books,' she called. 'I hope we win something.'

Adam Hope got out of the Land-rover, his vet's bag in his hand. Mandy watched as Gran had a quick word with her son. Then she turned to her mum.

'What's the raffle for?' she asked.

'The church roof fund,' Mrs Hope said. 'The vicar

has been collecting prizes for it all week. It's going to be drawn on Friday afternoon at the church bazaar.' She looked at her tickets. 'What's the betting I win the prize I donated?'

Mandy laughed. 'What did you donate?' she said.

'A food hamper,' Mrs Hope said.

'Oh well,' said Mandy. 'It would save you a trip to the supermarket.'

Mrs Hope's eyes were on Gran.

'Gran's on the warpath again,' Mandy said.

Mrs Hope nodded. She looked concerned. 'So are quite a lot of other people,' she replied. 'And Mr Barber only arrived yesterday!'

'Mr Barber?' said Mandy. 'Is that the man who's running the post office?'

Mrs Hope nodded. 'I think we're going to hear quite a lot of complaints about Mr Barber,' she said. Then she shrugged. 'Maybe he'll settle down soon, get the feel of the place.' She smiled. 'That's enough about Mr Barber,' she said. 'How is Cally?'

'She's great, Mum,' said Mandy. Then she paused.

Emily Hope looked carefully at her. 'Anything wrong?' she said.

Mandy bit her lip. 'Not exactly *wrong*,' she said.

Mrs Hope looked concerned.

'It's just that Penny and her mum are going away for the weekend and Mr Hapwell is awfully busy.' Mandy cast a glance at her mum.

'And . . .' Mrs Hope said with a twinkle in her eye.

'And Penny said Gussie will get awfully lonely without her,' Mandy said.

'Aha!' said Mrs Hope.

Mandy grinned in spite of herself.

'Aha, what?' she said.

Emily Hope raised her eyebrows. 'You've got something to tell me,' she said.

Mandy shook her head in disbelief. 'How do you know?' she said.

But Mrs Hope only smiled. Mandy laughed. It was never any good trying to keep secrets from her mum. She always knew.

Mr Hope came back up the path. 'Gran's got a bee in her bonnet,' he said. Then he looked from Mandy to his wife. 'I'm just going in to do the medications,' he said and gave Mandy a wink. 'See you later, Mandy – maybe.'

'Coward!' Mandy called after him. Then she turned to her mother.

'Now,' said Emily Hope. 'Exactly when are you planning to bring Gussie home?'

* * *

'Yippee!' Mandy yelled as she raced into the residential unit.

'Got to go! Got to go!' croaked a parrot hoarsely from a cage halfway down the rank.

Mandy shoved a finger through the bars and tickled it under the chin. The parrot ruffled its bright green and yellow feathers and stared up at her mournfully. 'You aren't well enough to go yet, Pippa,' Mandy said. 'Fancy getting a stone stuck in your crop. Silly bird!'

Mr Hope turned from replacing the dressing on a puppy's neck. 'She's making a good recovery,' he said, looking at Pippa.

Mandy shook her head. Mr Hope had had to perform a delicate operation to get the stone out. 'Maybe that'll teach her to be careful what she eats in future,' Mandy said.

Mr Hope shook his head. 'Chance would be a fine thing,' he said. 'Pippa will try anything once.'

Mandy grinned and came to stand beside him at the treatment table. She looked down at the puppy. He was a three-month-old bulldog and Mandy had already fallen in love with him. He had a wrinkly little face, a glossy brown coat and eyes that looked like melted chocolate drops.

'How is Jack?' she said anxiously.

Mr Hope gave her a reassuring smile. 'His wound is healing nicely,' he said. 'We'll be able to take the stitches out at the end of the week.'

Mandy stroked the puppy's back and he wagged his stumpy tail and tried to roll over. 'Poor Jack,' she said. 'He really was miserable when he came in.'

Mr Hope looked at the puppy. 'He's a brave little thing,' he said. 'But he isn't big enough to cope with Tom yet.'

Mandy nodded. Tom was Walter Pickard's black and white cat. Tom was shaped like a barrel and he was a bully to boot. And Tom wasn't afraid of any dog – especially not a little puppy.

'Poor Jack was just trying to be friendly,' Mandy said. 'He has such a trusting nature. He'll know better from now on. He must be looking forward to going home.'

Mr Hope didn't say anything. Mandy looked at him. 'Dad?' she said. 'Is anything wrong?'

Mr Hope picked Jack up gently. 'I'm afraid Jack can't go home, Mandy,' he said.

'Why not?' said Mandy.

Mr Hope frowned. 'His owner is going abroad,' he said. 'A new job. And he can't take a dog.'

'So what's going to happen to Jack?' Mandy said.

Mr Hope shrugged. 'I suppose we'll have to hand

him over to Betty Hilder's animal sanctuary when he's well again,' he said.

Mandy frowned. 'Then we'll never know who his new owner will be,' she said.

Mr Hope handed her the little puppy. 'I'm afraid there's nothing else we can do,' he said.

Mandy cradled Jack in her arms. 'Poor Jack,' she said. 'He'd make a perfect pet for the right person. He's so lovable.'

The puppy stuck out his rough pink tongue and licked her hand. Mandy settled him gently back in his cage and latched the door.

'I'll take him over to Betty's next week,' said Mr Hope.

Mandy looked at the puppy. Already his eyes were closing in sleep. He was such a placid little thing, and he looked adorable with his head resting on his paws. He started to make little bubbling noises. Mandy laughed. 'He's snoring!' she said.

Suddenly it seemed impossible just to send him to the animal sanctuary, though, of course, Betty Hilder would look after him well.

'Maybe I can think of something else,' said Mandy.

'Like what?' said Mr Hope.

Mandy frowned. 'I don't know,' she said. 'I'll need to think about it.'

Mr Hope laughed. 'You're going to try to find somebody in Welford to take him aren't you?' he said.

Mandy thought of Toby and Mrs Ponsonby. 'I've done it before,' she replied, grinning.

Mr Hope shook his head. 'You're a one-person pet placement agency!' he said.

Mandy tossed her hair back. 'I like that,' she said. 'But it's a two-person agency. James helps.'

'Speaking of James and persuading people to take animals in,' Mr Hope said, 'I take it you've had good news.'

Mandy grinned. 'Mum says so long as it's only for the weekend we can have Gussie here – provided . . .'

Mr Hope finished the sentence for her. 'Provided you look after her,' he said. 'You know the rules, Mandy. Your mum and I are too busy with the practice to look after your waifs and strays.'

Mandy smiled. 'I know that,' she said.

'We'll have to keep Gussie in a separate pen to avoid cross infection with the other animals,' Mr Hope went on.

Mandy nodded. Cross infection was a real danger and keeping farm animals and wild animals separate from domestic pets was a sensible precaution.

'I'll ring James after tea,' she said. 'He'll help me.'

'And I'll run you up to Twyford on Friday afternoon,' Mr Hope said. 'I want to check on Titan in a couple of days. It *was* ringworm and a pretty bad case of it. Anyway, you'd never get a goose on the back of your bike.'

Mandy grinned. She turned to the animal cages. 'Thanks, Dad,' she said. 'Now, what can I do to help?'

Mandy loved helping out at medication time. It was so good to see the animals making progress. There were two tiny premature kittens in the residential unit that she was particularly fond of. They were being fed on Vita-milk to strengthen them but they needed some vitamin supplement as well. Mandy carefully measured out some vitamin supplement into a dropper and checked the amount with Mr Hope.

'Perfect,' he said. 'Just make sure they swallow it. I'll hold the kittens and you do the drops.'

Mr Hope opened the kittens' cage and gently lifted out the first of them. Mandy cupped the kitten's head in her hand and rubbed his throat gently just under the chin. The kitten obediently opened his mouth and Mandy inserted the dropper and squeezed. The kitten looked mildly surprised. Mandy continued to rub his throat gently, encouraging him to swallow.

'Well done, Mandy,' Mr Hope said. 'Now the next one.'

Mandy flushed with pleasure. Getting animals to take their medication wasn't easy, especially when they were as tiny as these kittens.

Mandy took a fresh dropper and repeated the process with the other kitten. 'There,' she said as she put the second kitten back in his cage. 'And be good.'

The kitten looked up at her and yawned, his tiny pink tongue flicking out.

'I think he likes those vitamins,' Mandy laughed.

Mandy and Mr Hope made the rounds of the remaining cages. There was a gerbil with a runny eye that was responding well to eye drops and a rabbit with a bad ear infection.

Mandy rubbed in some antiseptic ointment and held the rabbit while Mr Hope administered an antibiotic injection.

'That should do it,' he said. 'But I think we'll keep this one for a few days more.'

Mandy placed the rabbit back in his cage. He was certainly looking very sorry for himself.

When Mrs Hope called them for tea Mandy was just finishing bandaging a hamster's leg.

'You've made a good job of that,' Mr Hope said as

they washed their hands. 'We'll make a vet of you yet!'

Mandy smiled. 'It's what I want to be,' she said. 'I want to be just like you and Mum.' She knew it would take a lot of effort and years of study but, as she looked round the residential unit, she knew it was worth it if she could spend her life helping animals.

Mandy and James hurtled into Animal Ark on Friday at lunch-time. Blackie lolloped at their heels.

'Hey, what's the panic?' Jean Knox said from behind the reception desk.

Mandy grinned and James shoved his glasses up his nose.

'It's mid-term break,' James said.

'And we're going to collect Gussie this afternoon, Jean,' said Mandy. 'Dad's taking us up there.'

'We thought we'd take Blackie,' James said.

Blackie jumped up and put his front paws on James's chest.

'Down Blackie,' James said.

Blackie looked at him soulfully and stayed right where he was.

'Maybe that isn't such a good idea,' said Mandy, laughing.

Jean looked at them over the top of her glasses. 'I

heard about you going to collect the goose,' she said. 'But your dad is busy at the moment.' Jean looked worriedly towards the surgery door. 'In fact they all are. Your mum, your dad and Simon.'

Simon was the practice nurse. If they were all busy in the surgery there must be some emergency.

Mandy felt her heart turn over. An emergency that took two vets and a nurse to deal with could only mean one thing. There was an animal in serious trouble!

# Three

'What's happened, Jean?' Mandy said. 'What's wrong?'

'It's that Mr Barber from the post office,' Jean said.

Mandy and James looked at each other.

'Mr Barber?' said Mandy. 'Does he have a pet? What kind of pet? Is it sick?'

Jean pursed her lips. 'No,' she said. 'Mr Barber does *not* have a pet.' She shook her head so violently that her glasses fell off and bounced on the chain round her neck. 'And, if you ask me,' she went on, 'that man isn't fit to have anything to do with animals – whatsoever!'

Mandy was astonished. She had never seen Jean so annoyed with anyone.

'What do you mean?' she asked.

Jean didn't get a chance to answer. There was a crash as the surgery door flew open. Blackie jumped with fright. Mandy and James whirled round. Adam and Emily Hope were standing on one side of the examination table, Simon on the other. He looked really worried. But it was another man who had flung open the door. He was small and tubby and his face was bright red with anger.

'And if you won't do anything about it, I'll ring the police!' he shouted.

Mandy barely looked at him. Her eyes were on the dog that he had by the collar. It was a young German Shepherd.

'Sheba!' she said and the dog turned at the sound of her voice.

Mr Barber yanked its collar and Sheba yelped.

At once Mandy was across the room. 'Don't do that,' she said. 'You're hurting her.'

Mr Barber turned to her. He wasn't much taller than she was. 'Another one!' he said, seeing Blackie. 'You keep that animal away from me.' He turned back to Mr Hope. 'I've no time for all this nonsense,' he yelled. 'That dog bit me. It should be put down –

now!' He pointed a finger at Mr Hope. 'And if you won't do it, we'll just have to see what the police say.'

Mandy took a step backwards and looked at the man, horrified.

'You can't do that,' she said. 'Sheba isn't even your dog. She belongs to Mr Moon. And she would never bite anybody.'

Mandy sank to her knees and put her arms round Sheba's neck. Mr Barber let go of Sheba's collar and the dog snuggled close to Mandy. The German Shepherd belonged to Mr Moon, a local artist. She had been treated at Animal Ark when her leg was broken in a road accident. You couldn't find a nicer or gentler dog.

Mrs Hope moved towards Mandy. 'It's all right, Mandy,' she said. 'We've explained all that to Mr Barber. But if he says Sheba bit him then he has a right to report it to the police.'

Mandy looked up, tears forming in her eyes. 'I don't believe it,' she said. 'Sheba would never do a thing like that. And where's Mr Moon?'

Mr Hope looked puzzled. 'That's a good question,' he said. 'Sheba seems to have been out on her own.'

'Mr Moon never lets Sheba wander round the village on her own,' said James.

'I don't understand,' said Mandy. 'Where did you find Sheba, Mr Barber? What happened?'

Mr Barber's lips twitched impatiently. 'That animal is dangerous,' he said, pointing at Sheba. 'I was loading supplies into the shed at the back of the post office and it leaped over the wall and tried to savage me.'

'It did nothing of the sort,' said a deep voice from the door.

Everybody turned. It was Walter Pickard, his kindly face creased with concern.

'How do you know?' Mr Barber yelled. 'It's none of your business anyway.'

'It's my business when you're accusing a poor defenceless animal,' said Walter. 'And I came right along here as fast as I could when I saw you dragging Sheba off.' He looked round at everybody. 'I was passing the lane at the back of the post office and I saw what happened. Sheba was pulling at Mr Barber's sleeve and he was trying to shake her off. But if that dog was trying to savage anybody then I'm a monkey's uncle!'

Mr Barber held out his hand. 'And what do you call this then?' he said.

Mandy looked at his hand. She couldn't see anything. 'What?' she said, puzzled.

'That,' said Mr Barber, pointing to a tiny scratch on the back of his hand.

'The way you were shaking Sheba off and yelling at her, I'm surprised that's all you got,' said Walter Pickard. 'That's an intelligent dog and the way she was trying to pull you, I'd say she had something she wanted to tell you.'

Mandy leaped to her feet. 'Mr Moon's house is quite near the post office,' she said.

'What if something has happened to him?' said James.

'That's just what I'm beginning to wonder, young man,' Walter Pickard said.

'Maybe we should go round and see,' Mandy said.

Mr Hope looked at his watch. 'There's only half an hour of surgery left,' he said to Mrs Hope. 'Simon and I can manage here.'

Mrs Hope was halfway out of the surgery already. 'We'll go there right now,' she said briskly. 'And I suggest that you come with us, Mr Barber. If you have any accusations to make, you should make them to the dog's owner first.'

Mandy looked at Mrs Hope. Her voice had sounded really stern, not like her usual voice at all. She was such a gentle person. But Mr Barber deserved it, Mandy was sure of that.

She was even more sure when they got to Moon Cottage. Mr Moon lived at the top of one of the narrow alleyways that ran off the High Street. There was a terrace of three stone houses with black tiled roofs and small mullioned windows. Moon Cottage had a crescent-shaped doorknocker with a painting of a half moon below it. There was no answer when they rapped on the door with the doorknocker. Mrs Hope pushed gently and the door swung open.

'Hello!' called Mandy. 'Anybody there?'

'In here,' said a voice from the sitting-room.

Mandy, James, Mrs Hope and Mr Barber walked towards the sitting-room. Blackie kept close to James. He obviously didn't trust Mr Barber. But Sheba made straight for the sound of her master's voice.

The door was open and Mr Moon was lying at an awkward angle on the floor. Sheba trotted to his side and lay down beside him. Mr Moon put out a hand and stroked Sheba's head.

'Ah, it's the young lady from Animal Ark,' he said as Mandy came in. 'How very pleased I am to see you. And I see you have brought some friends.'

Mandy looked at Mr Moon. His face looked pale against his black hair and beard and the bright blue scarf at the open neck of his shirt made his piercing blue eyes even bluer. His mouth was tight, as if he was in pain. But even so he was still his funny old-fashioned self. His voice was always kind and gentle even though he sometimes looked quite stern.

'Oh, Mr Moon,' she said. 'Are you hurt?'

Mr Moon smiled then grimaced. 'A twisted ankle,' he said. 'But I'm afraid I cannot seem to get up. Stupid of me.'

Sheba licked his face and Mr Moon put up a hand and rubbed her ears.

'Clever girl,' he said. He looked up at all of them. 'I sent her for help,' he said. 'She really is a most intelligent dog. Which one of you did she find?'

'Mr Barber,' Mandy said. 'She went to the post office.'

Mr Moon looked at Mr Barber. 'And you brought my friends to help me, Mr Barber,' Mr Moon said. 'That was very kind of you. How can I thank you?'

Mr Barber's face was as red as a beetroot. 'You can keep that dog away from me!' he spluttered. 'Fetching help indeed. Stuff and nonsense. If I see that animal running wild again, I'll report it to the police!'

Sheba looked up at Mr Barber's angry voice. She gave a low growl.

'See what I mean?' said Mr Barber, taking a quick

step back. 'That dog is dangerous. Just you keep it away from me!'

And before anybody could say anything else he had turned on his heel and was gone.

'Well, honestly,' said James. 'How rotten can you get? Imagine calling Sheba dangerous when all she did was try to help Mr Moon.'

But Mandy was staring at the door. A thought had occurred to her – a very surprising thought.

'What is it?' said James, looking at her face.

Mandy turned to him. 'I don't think he was just being rotten to Sheba,' she said. 'I think it's more than that. I think he hates dogs because he's scared of them.'

Mandy sat in the back seat of the Land-rover as it wound its way up Twyford Hill. The vale spread out below them, the fields and houses looked like something out of a toy landscape.

'I still don't think being frightened of dogs is any excuse for being so rotten to Sheba,' James said. He bent down and gave Blackie a pat. 'You'd go for help if I was in trouble, wouldn't you, Blackie?'

Blackie jumped up at James and wagged his tail.

'Ouch!' said Mr Hope from the front seat of the Land-rover. Blackie's tail had caught him a hefty wallop.

'Sorry,' said James. 'Lie down, Blackie.'

Blackie tried to climb on to James's lap. As much as James tried to train Blackie, he was one disobedient dog.

Mandy shook her head. 'Mr Barber didn't want to believe it,' she said. 'How can anybody dislike animals so much?'

They were on their way to Twyford to pick up Gussie.

'Nearly there,' said Mr Hope. 'Have you got the travelling cage ready?'

'It's here,' said Mandy. 'I hope it's big enough.' She looked doubtfully at the wire-mesh cage lined with fresh newspaper.

'Gussie is a pretty big goose,' said James. 'And nearly as naughty as Blackie.'

Blackie barked, hearing his name.

They turned on to the farm track and rattled over the cattle grid. Up ahead Mandy could see the cattle shed and the barn beside it. There was smoke coming from the chimney of the old farmhouse on the opposite side of the farmyard. On their left as they approached the farmyard was the goose enclosure.

Mandy looked at their long necks and strong bills. She was glad they were going to look after Gussie. It

would be no fun being pecked at by a flock of geese.
And Gussie was used to a lot of attention. No doubt
she would miss Penny a lot.

'Hello, there!' called Tom Hapwell as they turned
into the farmyard. He looked worried.

'What's up, Tom?' said Mr Hope. 'Is it the bull?'

Tom Hapwell scratched his head. 'As if that wasn't
bad enough,' he said. 'The ringworm doesn't seem
to be clearing up and I'm scared of it spreading to
the rest of the cattle though I've isolated Titan. And,
now it looks as if my best herd has got the spring
staggers.'

Mandy frowned. Spring staggers affected cows that
had been moved outdoors to graze. It was caused
by the change of feeding from concentrates and
silage to rich new grass. The staggers could be really
serious if the cattle didn't get the proper treatment
in time. Animals had been known to collapse and
injure themselves really badly.

'I'll have a look at them,' said Mr Hope, getting
down from the Land-rover. 'Let's go.'

'Oh, Mr Hapwell,' Mandy said. 'We've come to
collect Gussie.'

Tom Hapwell turned to her. 'Oh, yes,' he said.
'You'll find her round the back. I told Penny to put
her in the pen before she and her mum left. Penny

was so relieved that you'll be looking after Gussie this weekend.' He grinned. 'She's left a list of instructions for you as long as your arm. You'll find it on the kitchen table. Don't mind the spelling, now.'

'We won't,' said Mandy, laughing.

'Sorry we're a bit late,' said James.

'That's all right,' said Mr Hapwell. 'Just you go on and get her now.' He scratched his head again and turned to Mr Hope. 'It's been one thing after another. First getting Penny and her mum away, then the vicar arriving and now spring staggers – not to mention the bull.'

'Uh-oh,' said James as he and Mandy watched Tom Hapwell and Mr Hope stride away towards the cattle shed. 'It seems like we've come at a bad time.'

Mandy shrugged. 'Well, Dad's welcome anyway,' she said, 'And we'll be saving Mr Hapwell a bit of work looking after Gussie. Come on, let's get her.'

Mandy and James lugged the travelling cage round to the back garden of the farmhouse. It had handles at each end as well as on the top so it was easy enough to carry – when it was empty. It would be a different matter when Gussie was in it.

'There's the pen,' said James.

As they walked towards the pen, Mandy frowned.

'Can you see her?' she said.

James shook his head. 'Maybe she's in there,' he said, pointing to a miniature shed, something like a kennel, that stood in the corner of the pen.

Mandy unlatched the pen gate and started calling Gussie's name. There was no answering honk.

'Have a look in the shed,' James suggested.

Mandy walked softly over to the little shed. She didn't want to alarm Gussie. But there was still no sound. She bent and peered inside. 'It's empty,' she said.

'So where's Gussie?' said James.

Mandy looked at him. 'She must have got out.

Penny said she sometimes manages to get out of her pen.'

James grinned. 'It's a goose hunt,' he said. He looked down at Blackie. 'Find Gussie, Blackie,' he said. 'Come on, find!'

Blackie looked up at him, his pink tongue hanging out.

Mandy laughed. 'Good try, James.' She looked around the farmyard. 'Oh, well,' she said. 'Gussie can't have gone far. Let's look for her.'

They looked everywhere. In the barn, in the dairy, even in the house. They found the list of instructions Penny had left for them in the kitchen. It was written in large childish letters and it *was* nearly as long as Mandy's arm. It was mostly a list of what Gussie liked to eat.

'Is there anything that isn't on that list?' James said.

Mandy laughed. 'Geese eat anything,' she said. 'Mostly grain and any kind of fruit and vegetables as well as grass and plants. They aren't fussy.'

'That's a relief anyway,' said James. 'We won't have any difficulty feeding her – if we find her.'

But there was no trace of Gussie.

'Where do you think she is?' said James as they came back out into the farmyard.

Mandy shook her head. Then she looked over towards the goose enclosure. 'You don't think she's in there with the others, do you?' she said.

James looked at the geese. 'There must be thirty or forty geese in there,' he said. 'And I don't fancy trying to check them all. Anyway, how would she get in?'

'You know what Penny said,' Mandy replied. 'Gussie is quite an adventurous goose.'

James sighed. 'OK,' he said. 'But let's check from this side of the fence. After all, Gussie shouldn't be too hard to spot if she *is* in there. She's got that dark wing, remember?'

Mandy nodded. 'You take the left-hand side of the enclosure, I'll take the right.'

It took a while to check because, of course, the geese wouldn't stay still. But none of the geese in the enclosure had one dark wing.

'She isn't there,' James said.

'So where on earth can she be?' Mandy said, puzzled. 'Let's go and see if Mr Hapwell knows.'

They found Tom Hapwell coming out of the cattle shed with Mr Hope. He stopped to check the contents of a grain bin standing just inside the shed.

'Keep an eye on the bull,' Mr Hope was saying. 'The ringworm is proving quite resistant so don't let him near any of the other animals. And keep an eye on that herd as well. Those pellets I gave you for the feed should clear it up.'

Mandy and James looked at each other. It didn't seem a very good time to present Mr Hapwell with another problem but what else could they do?

'Hi, you two,' said Mr Hope. 'Where's Gussie?'

'We couldn't find her,' said Mandy. She looked at Mr Hapwell.

'But she was in her pen,' said Mr Hapwell. 'I saw her there earlier.'

'Well, she isn't there now,' said James.

Mr Hapwell looked puzzled. Then he clapped a hand to his forehead. 'Oh, no!' he said, his face going pale.

'What?' said Mandy.

'The vicar, Mr Hadcroft,' said Mr Hapwell. 'He came to collect a goose. I said I'd give him one for a prize in the church roof fund raffle.'

'You didn't give him Gussie?' said James.

'*I* didn't give him *any* of them,' said Tom Hapwell. 'I was up in the top field looking at the herd. I sent him down here to get one for himself.'

'But why would he take Gussie?' said Mandy.

Tom Hapwell looked worried. 'I told him to take one from the enclosure,' he said.

'So do you think Mr Hadcroft thought you meant Gussie's enclosure?'

Tom Hapwell ran a hand through his hair. 'It's possible,' he said. 'I don't think he knew about Penny's pet goose. He might have thought I'd put Gussie in the pen for him.'

'That's OK. We'll get her back from Mr Hadcroft,' said James.

'That's right,' said Mr Hapwell. 'You get Gussie back and tell Mr Hadcroft he can come and get another goose.' He dipped a hand in the grain bin. 'You'd better take some grain to keep her happy,' he said. 'Gussie can be a bit of a handful sometimes.'

Mandy grinned and held out her hand for the grain. 'Thanks, Mr Hapwell,' she said, stuffing it in her jeans pocket. 'Don't worry. We won't let Penny down.'

Tom Hapwell spread his hands. 'I'd come with you but . . .'

'I know,' said Mandy. 'You've got enough to do here.'

'Don't worry,' said James. 'There's no problem.'

Mr Hope raised his eyebrows.

'Or is there a problem?' said Mandy.

'Only that the raffle is this afternoon,' said Mr Hope. 'Don't you remember? It's due to be drawn at three o'clock – after the church bazaar.'

'Oh, no,' said Mandy, looking at her watch. 'It's quarter to three already. We've got to get there before the raffle is drawn.'

'And Gussie gets given away as a prize,' said James.

'Hop in the Land-rover,' Mr Hope said. 'I'll drop you off at the church. I've got a call to make at Mr Matthews' dairy farm. His son has gone to Australia and he has to run the farm on his own for a month or two. I said I would pop in. But I can just about afford the time for a detour.'

'Right,' said Mandy. 'Come on, James.'

'Blackie!' James yelled. 'Heel!'

Blackie wagged his tail and barked from the other end of the farmyard.

'Oh, all right,' said James and went to get him.

'Come on, James!' Mandy called, getting into the Land-rover. 'We've got to go!'

She watched as James clipped Blackie's lead on and began to run towards the Land-rover. They would be in time, she thought. They had to be.

# Four

Mandy found herself leaning forward, trying to make the Land-rover go faster.

'Hurry, Dad!' she said.

Mr Hope kept his eyes on the road. 'I'm going as fast as it's safe to go,' he said reprovingly.

Mandy bit her lip. 'Sorry,' she said. 'It's just that we have to get there before the raffle is drawn.'

'We'll get there,' said Mr Hope. 'Safely.'

Mandy looked at James and he smiled sympathetically. 'I know how you feel,' he said. 'But your dad is right.'

But that didn't help Mandy. She couldn't

remember the journey from Twyford to Welford taking so long.

At last the church was in sight. Mandy was on her feet almost before the Land-rover had stopped moving.

'Thanks, Dad!' she called over her shoulder as she leaped out in front of the church.

'Good luck,' Mr Hope called back. 'I've got to dash. I'll see you later.'

Mandy and James waved as Mr Hope turned the Land-rover and drove off.

'There's Mr Hadcroft,' James said. 'He's just coming out of the church.'

Mandy turned. Mr Hadcroft, the vicar, was coming down the path. Mandy liked Mr Hadcroft. He had dark curly hair and a sense of humour. He was always teasing her. He also had a tabby cat called Jemima.

'Mr Hadcroft!' Mandy shouted. She flew through the lychgate and up the path to the church.

'Hey, where's the fire?' Mr Hadcroft joked.

Mandy grinned and came to a halt in front of him.

James, behind Mandy, couldn't stop quickly enough and cannoned into her.

Mr Hadcroft looked from one to the other.

'You haven't drawn the raffle for the church roof fund yet, have you, Mr Hadcroft?' Mandy said.

Mr Hadcroft beamed. 'We made nearly four hundred pounds in ticket sales,' he said. 'Of course, we had very generous donations for prizes, like your mother's food hamper, Mandy. The ladies are still counting up the takings from the bazaar. I must say, it's been a very successful afternoon all round.'

James interrupted. 'You see, you took the wrong goose,' he said.

'It wasn't your fault,' Mandy added quickly. 'You took little Penny Hapwell's pet goose by mistake.'

'So if you give us Gussie back, you can have any other goose you like from Twyford. Mr Hapwell says so,' James finished breathlessly.

Mr Hadcroft frowned. 'Wait a moment,' he said seriously. 'Let me get this straight. Are you saying I took Penny's pet goose for a raffle prize?'

Mandy nodded. 'But it's all right. You can have another,' she said. Then her voice trailed away as she saw Mr Hadcroft's face.

'Has the raffle been drawn?' James asked.

Mr Hadcroft nodded. 'And won,' he said. 'The goose and all the other prizes are gone.'

Mandy shrugged. 'That's still OK,' she said. 'We can get her back.'

James bit his lip. 'It wasn't somebody from outside Welford, was it?' he said.

Mandy gasped. What if the person who won Gussie lived in York – or even farther away? What if they had just been passing through and there was no way to contact them? Panic seized her as she thought of Penny.

But Mr Hadcroft was shaking his head. 'No,' he said. 'It was someone from the village.'

Mandy let out a great sigh of relief. 'Thank goodness for that,' she said. 'Who was it, Mr Hadcroft?'

Mr Hadcroft's face still looked worried. He looked from Mandy to James. 'Mr Barber won the goose,' he said. 'You know, the temporary postmaster.'

Mandy's heart sank. 'Mr Barber!' she said.

She looked at James. She could see he was thinking the same thing. They would have to go and ask Mr Barber to give Gussie back. And after the business with Sheba, Mandy and James were very definitely not Mr Barber's favourite people.

'Uh-oh, said James. 'This could be tricky.'

'Look,' said Mr Hadcroft. 'Why don't you come over to the vicarage and I'll ring Mr Barber and explain things. I'm sure we'll get this sorted out.'

'Oh, would you, Mr Hadcroft?' Mandy said.

Mr Hadcroft smiled. 'No trouble at all,' he said.

'And anyway, I want you to see how well Jemima is doing.'

Jemima, Mr Hadcroft's tabby cat, had recently had to have part of her tail removed after an accident.

'Blackie!' James called.

For once Blackie came when he was called. James looked surprised.

'Let's hope he behaves well when he seen Jemima,' James said.

They began to walk towards the vicarage. Blackie raced ahead, then doubled back on himself, then chased his tail, then lolloped up to them looking for admiration.

Mr Hadcroft laughed and bent down to give the Labrador a pat. Mandy watched him and an idea formed in her mind.

'Mr Hadcroft, you like animals, don't you,' she said.

Mr Hadcroft looked surprised. 'Of course I do,' he answered.

'I mean, you're really fond of Jemima,' Mandy went on. She could feel James looking at her. He raised his eyebrows and his glasses slid right down to the end of his nose. He knew she was up to something.

Mandy bit her lip. 'I bet you like dogs as well,' she said.

'Mmm,' said Mr Hadcroft.

'Come on, Mandy, spit it out. We know you're up to something,' James said.

Mandy looked at Mr Hadcroft. He was grinning.

'OK,' she said. 'It's just that there's this absolutely adorable bulldog puppy at Animal Ark just now.'

'And it just happens to be looking for a home,' Mr Hadcroft said.

Mandy nodded.

Mr Hadcroft smiled. 'I'll ask around,' he said. 'We're sure to come up with someone.'

Mandy was disappointed. 'I thought perhaps you might like a puppy,' she said.

Mr Hadcroft looked genuinely sorry. 'I would,' he said. 'But you know what Jemima is like about the vicarage. She regards it as very much her own territory. I don't think she'd take kindly to a puppy.'

Mr Hadcroft was right, Mandy thought, as they approached the vicarage. Jemima probably wouldn't be happy with another animal sharing her home.

They trooped into Mr Hadcroft's little kitchen. There was a cat basket by the stove and curled up in it was a ball of tabby fur. As they came into the room, the ball of fur stirred and two wide eyes looked at them.

'Jemima!' said Mandy. She went to pick up the

tabby cat, burying her face in her soft fur.

Jemima looked suspiciously at Blackie but her fur settled down as Mandy spoke to her and she began to purr.

'I'll phone Mr Barber,' Mr Hadcroft said. 'We'll soon get this sorted out.'

Mandy sat on a chair by the window with Jemima on her lap. She hooked the window cord over and dangled it in front of Jemima. The cat batted it playfully with her front paws. But Mandy's mind was on other things.

'What will we do if Mr Barber won't give Gussie back?' she said.

James looked shocked. 'Don't be daft,' he said. 'Of course he'll give her back. I mean she's Penny's pet. Nobody could be rotten enough to keep someone else's pet.'

Mandy looked at James's outraged face. He was right, of course. Nobody could be mean enough to refuse to give a little girl's pet back.

There was a sound at the door and Mr Hadcroft came in. Mandy looked up eagerly, then her face fell as she saw the vicar's expression.

'What did Mr Barber say?' she said.

Mr Hadcroft spread his hands. 'I tried my best,' he said. 'But Mr Barber refuses to return Gussie.

He says he won the goose fair and square and he's keeping her.'

'But he can't,' wailed Mandy.

Mr Hadcroft shook his head. 'The trouble is he's perfectly within his rights. I can't make him give Gussie back. He won the raffle and the goose was the prize.'

'But did you explain that Gussie was Penny's pet?' asked James.

Mr Hadcroft nodded. 'Mr Barber says he can't stand all this sentimentality over animals. An animal is an animal and that's the end of it – that's what he says.' Mr Hadcroft ran a hand through his curly hair. 'I'm really sorry,' he said. 'I tried my best to reason with him but I can't force him to give Gussie up.'

'So what do we do?' said James. 'What on earth are we going to tell Penny?'

'Nothing,' said Mandy, her mouth set in a firm line.

'What?' said James.

Mandy stood up and set Jemima down on the floor. She fixed James with a determined look.

'We're going to see Mr Barber and we're going to make him give Gussie back,' she said.

'But he'll never give her to us,' said James. 'Not if he wouldn't hand her over to Mr Hadcroft.'

Mandy drew herself up. 'Mr Barber doesn't like animals,' she said. 'And he doesn't like us either. But if he thinks I'm just going to stand back and let him upset Penny he's got another think coming.' She looked at James. 'I'll go by myself if I have to,' she finished.

But James was on his feet. 'I'm with you,' he said. He looked down at Blackie. The Labrador thumped his tail on the floor, his pink tongue hanging out. 'And so is Blackie.'

'Good for you,' Mr Hadcroft said. 'Never give up – that's the way to succeed.'

James looked at Mandy. 'I almost feel sorry for Mr Barber,' he said. 'Not liking animals.'

Mandy snorted. 'Well, I don't,' she replied. 'And I'm going to make sure he knows it!'

# Five

'What's going on?' said James as they approached the post office.

They could hear angry voices coming from the shop.

'It sounds like an argument,' Mandy said.

James nodded. 'If Mr Barber is around, I'm not surprised. He seems to argue with everybody.'

'That sounds like Ernie Bell,' Mandy said.

Ernie Bell was a church bell-ringer along with her grandad and Walter Pickard. He was a retired carpenter and lived a few doors down from Walter in the row of cottages behind the Fox and Goose. He had a pet squirrel named Sammy and a cat called

Tiddles. He wasn't the easiest person to get on with but Mandy had never heard him shouting at anyone.

Mandy pushed open the door of the post office. She loved this shop; it was like Aladdin's Cave. You could buy all kinds of things there. There were big glass jars of mint humbugs and aniseed balls and other old-fashioned sweets on the shelves. It seemed that whenever you needed something, McFarlanes' would have it. And there was always a smile and a welcome from Mrs McFarlane. It was a shock to see Mr Barber behind the counter instead of the familiar figure of Mrs McFarlane in her blue gingham overall.

'Rules are rules!' Mr Barber was saying to Ernie Bell.

Ernie's face was red. He took off his cloth cap and rubbed his bristly grey hair. 'But I've told you. I've mixed up the labels on that parcel,' he said.

Mandy looked with interest at the walking-stick Ernie was carrying. She had never seen him with a walking-stick before.

Mr Barber shook his head. 'You shouldn't make mistakes,' he said. 'You should be more careful. You've handed over the parcel. Technically you've posted it. Now it has to be delivered – just as it is.' And he picked up a pipe and stuck it between his teeth.

'I've never heard such nonsense in my life!' said Ernie, banging his walking-stick on the floor. 'The parcel is lying there right in front of you. All you have to do is give it back to me. My little granddaughter is going to get a dumper truck for her birthday instead of the doll she wanted. And I've got to send the dumper truck to my grandson. If I don't get that parcel back little Emily will get the wrong present and Bobby won't get a present at all!'

Mr Barber drew himself up and puffed out his chest. He took his pipe out of his mouth and tapped the stem of it on the brown paper parcel lying on the counter on the other side of the grille. 'I've told you,' he said. 'Rules are rules. That's the trouble with people these days. They don't stick to the rules!'

Ernie Bell spluttered with anger. 'Mrs McFarlane wouldn't talk such nonsense,' he said.

Mr Barber leaned over the counter. 'Mrs McFarlane is not in charge of this post office for the time being,' he said. '*I* am. And I'm going to make sure that it's run properly. I don't hold with inefficiency and forgetfulness. And I don't hold with breaking the rules,' he finished.

Ernie Bell gave a final snort, clapped his cap back on his head, shook his stick at Mr Barber and stomped out of the post office.

'Hello, Mr Bell,' Mandy said as he passed.

Ernie looked at her. 'Harrumph!' he said. He jerked his head towards Mr Barber. 'I suppose Mr Perfect Postmaster *never* makes mistakes,' he said as he went out of the door.

Mandy turned to Mr Barber and her heart sank. He was stamping forms on the other side of the counter. He looked as if he was enjoying it. Stamp, *stamp*, STAMP, he went. Each stamp was louder than the last. His mouth was set in an angry line and his pipe was clenched tightly between his teeth. Things weren't looking too good. It certainly didn't seem to be the time to ask Mr Barber about Gussie. But they had no other choice.

'Mr Barber,' Mandy began.

Mr Barber looked up. 'Oh, it's you two,' he said. 'And what do you want? Don't you go touching anything now. I've got everything neat and tidy and I don't want you disarranging things.'

Mandy swallowed.

'It's about the raffle,' James said, plunging in.

'What about it?' said Mr Barber. Then he saw Blackie. 'And get that dog out of my post office,' he said. 'No dogs allowed.'

'But Mrs McFarlane never minds,' said James.

Mr Barber drew himself up and James took a step back.

'Who's in charge here?' he said. 'I said out and I *mean* out.'

Blackie looked up quickly at the tone of Mr Barber's voice. He was threatening James and Blackie didn't like that. He growled softly.

Mr Barber jumped. 'See what I mean!' he said. 'Vicious things, dogs. Get it out of here and don't bring it in again!'

Mandy couldn't help herself. 'It isn't an it, it's a *he*,' she said. 'And he only growled because you shouted at James. Blackie thought you were threatening him.'

Mr Barber took his pipe out of his mouth and rapped it on the counter. 'Threatening!' he shouted. 'So now it's threatening to tell somebody the rules, is it? You get that animal out of here and yourself with it. Troublemakers!'

Mandy looked at James and shrugged. James took Blackie's collar and pushed the Labrador out of the door. 'Stay!' he said and closed the door on Blackie.

Mandy looked closely at Mr Barber. He seemed to relax a little once Blackie had gone. Was Mr Barber really afraid of dogs? She dismissed the thought. How could anyone be afraid of Blackie? She took a deep breath.

'Mr Barber, we have to talk to you about the prize you won in the raffle,' she said.

'Can't you see I'm busy?' said Mr Barber, stamping away.

'But it's important,' said Mandy. 'You see, you got the wrong goose.'

'You were supposed to get a goose from Twyford Farm,' said James. 'But Mr Hadcroft made a mistake and took the wrong goose.'

'More mistakes!' said Mr Barber. 'This village is full of people who make mistakes!'

'Everybody makes mistakes sometimes,' said James.

Mr Barber stopped stamping his forms and looked up. '*I* don't,' he said. Then he started stamping again, louder than ever.

Mandy raised her voice. 'You got little Penny Hapwell's pet goose,' she said. 'She's called Gussie and we're supposed to be looking after her for Penny.'

'So if you give us Gussie back, we'll get you another goose,' said James.

'Or you can go and choose any one you like from Twyford Farm,' said Mandy. 'We've already spoken to Mr Hapwell.'

Mr Barber stopped stamping and looked at them through the grille. 'And what would I want to do that for?' he said. 'I've got a goose.'

'But that goose is Penny's pet,' said Mandy.

Mr Barber leaned towards them. 'I told the vicar and I'll tell you and anybody else that asks,' he said. 'I won that goose fair and square in the raffle. All according to the rules. I bought a ticket and I won the goose. It's mine and nobody else's. If people make mistakes they've only got themselves to blame. As for having a goose for a pet, I've never heard anything so stupid.'

'But you must give Gussie back,' Mandy said.

'Must?' said Mr Barber. 'There's no must about it. Rules are rules and I won that goose fair and square.'

'You wouldn't have if we'd got to Twyford in time,' James muttered.

'What's that?' said Mr Barber.

'That's right,' said Mandy. 'It was your fault we were late getting to Twyford. If you hadn't made all that fuss over Sheba, we would have got there before Penny and her mum left.'

Mr Barber looked at her. 'I haven't the faintest idea what you're talking about,' he said. 'And I don't want to know,' he added as Mandy opened her mouth. 'As for the dog that attacked me—'

'She didn't attack you,' Mandy interrupted. 'She was trying to get help for Mr Moon.'

'Nonsense,' said Mr Barber. 'I don't believe that for a minute. And I'm far too busy to be bothered with you two any more. Out!'

Mandy tried one last time. 'Just give us the goose, Mr Barber. Please.'

Mr Barber didn't even bother to reply.

Mandy sighed and turned towards the door. Then her face creased in puzzlement. 'Why don't you like animals, Mr Barber?' she asked.

Mr Barber looked up. 'Who said I didn't?' he asked. 'I like geese – to eat! And I intend to eat my goose for lunch this Sunday – with all the trimmings!'

Mandy felt her mouth fall open. What a horrible man!

'Come on, Mandy,' James said, bundling her out of the shop.

They stood together in front of the post office.

'Did you hear that?' said Mandy. 'He's going to eat Gussie!'

James shook his head. 'What can we do?' he said. His face brightened. 'Maybe Mr Hapwell could talk to him.'

Mandy shrugged. 'What good would that do?' she

said. 'You heard him. He said he'd say the same to anybody. Besides, Mr Hapwell is so busy at the moment. It's our responsibility. Or at least it's mine. I said I would look after Gussie. And the vicar is right, James. Mr Barber did win Gussie. He's got a right to keep her. At least as far as the rules go.' Mandy sighed. 'Oh, why did it have to be Mr Barber that won Gussie? Why couldn't it have been somebody else – anybody else?'

'If we'd got there in time this wouldn't have happened,' said James.

'It's Mr Barber's fault,' said Mandy. 'He was the one who kept us back.'

'So what are we going to do?' said James.

Mandy thought. 'Where do you think Gussie is?' she said.

James shook his head. 'I don't know,' he said.

Mandy looked even more thoughtful. 'Let's try to find her,' she said. 'Just for starters.'

'What do you mean, "just for starters"?' James said.

But Mandy was looking around. 'Where's Blackie?' she said.

James shoved his hair back and scratched his head. 'I told him to stay,' he said.

'You didn't expect him to listen, did you?' Mandy said.

'I suppose not,' said James. 'Let's try round the back of the post office.'

They made their way down the side of the shop and round the back.

Blackie was there. He looked up and wagged his tail when he saw them. Then he went back to what he was doing.

'Blackie!' James said. 'Come away from there!'

Blackie was snuffling at a loose plank in the store shed at the back of the post office. He looked up again and gave a short bark. There was a sound from inside the shed.

'What are you doing, Blackie?' Mandy said. Then she stopped as she realised what the sound was. A steady hissing was coming from the shed. Mandy bent down and squinted through the crack in the planking. The sound came again.

'She's in there, James!' Mandy said. 'Mr Barber has put her in the shed. It's Gussie.'

'But it'll be dark in there,' said James.

'Poor Gussie,' Mandy said. 'We've got to get her out!'

James went to the shed door. Mandy heard a rattling noise and looked up.

'Bad news. The door is padlocked,' James said.

Mandy rose and came to look. The wood of the

door was rotten but the padlock was new.

'He's locked Gussie in,' James said.

Mandy nodded. 'That sounds just like Mr Barber,' she said. She turned a determined face to James. 'At least we can give her something to eat.' She dug in her jeans pocket and brought out some of the grain that Mr Hapwell had given her.

'Here you are, Gussie,' she said, sprinkling it under the hole in the planking. She saw Gussie's orange bill come down and peck at the grain.

'She seems awfully hungry,' Mandy said. 'I hope Mr Barber realises how much geese can eat. I'm sure Gussie is used to getting all kinds of titbits from Penny. She must be miserable in there.'

James looked really worried. 'But what can we do about it?' he said.

Mandy shook her hair back from her face. 'There's only one thing to do,' she said. 'We have to get Gussie out of there and take her somewhere safe.'

'You mean steal her?' said James.

Mandy looked seriously at him. 'What else is there to do?' she said. 'I promised Penny I'd looked after Gussie. I can't go back on my word. If I've got to steal Gussie to keep my promise then I will!'

# Six

'All we have to do is hide her for two days – until Penny and her mum come home,' Mandy said. 'Even Mr Barber couldn't be so hard-hearted as to take Penny's goose away from her. Not when he sees how fond she is of Gussie.'

James didn't look convinced. 'I don't know about that,' he said. 'But you're right. We've got to get Gussie out of that dark shed.'

Mandy smiled. She could always depend on James. 'Thanks, James,' she said. 'I knew you'd help.'

James grinned and spread his hands. 'Did I have a choice?' he said.

But Mandy didn't reply. She was thinking. She bit

her lip in concentration. 'We've got to do it soon,' she said.

'Like when?' said James. 'We can't do it now. I mean Mr Barber could catch us. He keeps his stores in there.'

Mandy frowned. 'The sooner we do it the better,' she said. She looked at her watch and her face lit up. 'The post must be due to be picked up pretty soon. Mr Davis always comes with the mail van around this time. That will keep Mr Barber out of the way.'

'You mean we do it now?' said James.

Mandy nodded. 'There's no time like the present,' she said. 'And we might not get another chance.'

James thought for a moment. 'It might work,' he said. 'But we'd have to be quick.'

'Of course it'll work,' Mandy said. 'But we've got to make up our minds now. We won't have much time.'

'So while Mr Barber is busy with the postman, we get Gussie out,' James said. Then he looked worried. 'But the shed's locked.'

Mandy nodded. 'There's a loose plank though,' she said.

James grinned. 'And there's a stick over there,' he said. 'All we have to do is lever that plank free.'

Mandy frowned. 'But where will we hide Gussie once we get her out of there?' she said.

James looked worried again. 'Good question,' he said. 'Mr Barber is bound to suspect us when he finds that Gussie is missing.'

'So we can't take her to Animal Ark,' said Mandy.

'Or to my house,' James said.

There was the sound of an engine and Mandy peered round the corner of the shed. 'It's the post office van,' she said. 'We'll need to be quick. We can think about hiding Gussie once we've got her out.'

'Right,' said James. 'Just as soon as Mr Davis is safely in the post office, we start.'

Mandy drew her head back. 'That's him going in now,' she said. 'OK, James, let's go!'

But stealing Gussie away from Mr Barber wasn't as easy as they had thought. For one thing, Blackie thought they were playing a great game and kept trying to steal James's stick. Blackie was clearly puzzled. If James had a stick, why wasn't he throwing it? Blackie barked.

'Get off, Blackie,' James grunted. 'And keep quiet!'

At last James managed to get the stick wedged under the loose plank. He leaned on it. Nothing happened.

'I'll help,' said Mandy.

She leaned her weight on the stick. 'The plank is starting to give a little,' she said.

James gritted his teeth. 'Lean harder,' he said.

Mandy leaned all her weight on the stick. Suddenly, there was a crack – and the stick broke.

'Oh, no!' said Mandy, disappointment flooding through her. 'What do we do now?'

But James wasn't listening to her. James was looking past her towards the corner of the shed. Now Mandy could hear it too – the sound of footsteps coming down the side of the post office. She looked at James.

'Oh, no,' she said. 'Mr Barber!'

Mandy and James waited as the steps came nearer. There was nowhere to hide. At the very corner of the shed the footsteps halted. Then a figure came round the corner.

'Mr Bell,' Mandy breathed with relief.

'We thought you were Mr Barber,' James said.

Blackie rushed up to Ernie Bell and began licking his hand.

'Good lad,' Ernie Bell said to Blackie. Then he looked at Mandy and James. 'And what are you two young ones up to?' he said.

'We're trying to get Gussie out,' Mandy said.

Ernie looked puzzled.

'Penny Hapwell's pet goose,' James said.

'Mr Hadcroft took the wrong one for the raffle,' said Mandy.

'And Mr Barber won it,' said James.

'And now he won't give Gussie back,' finished Mandy. 'He says he's going to eat her.'

Ernie Bell looked at them. 'She's in that old shed, then?' he said.

Mandy nodded. 'We don't even know if she's got any food or water.'

'And she's in the dark,' said James.

'And you're rescuing her?' said Ernie Bell.

Mandy felt relieved. Ernie had said 'rescuing', not 'stealing'. Surely, if he thought they were doing something wrong he would have said 'stealing'.

She nodded. 'But the stick we were using to lever off this plank broke.'

'And we haven't got another one,' said James.

'And Mr Barber will be finished with the postman any minute,' said Mandy.

Ernie Bell looked at them and his face broke into a grin. 'Well, well,' he said. 'What a lot of problems.' He rubbed his chin. 'Let's see now . . .' he said, looking at his walking-stick. 'Here's a fine strong stick.' His eyes twinkled. 'I won it in the raffle this afternoon. It's a good sturdy one, isn't it?' And he handed the stick to James.

'Thanks, Mr Bell,' said James.

'And,' Ernie Bell went on, 'I might just take a walk round to the post office and have a chat with Bob Davis about getting my parcel back. Making sure Mr Barber is there as well, of course,' he said. Ernie's eyes twinkled again.

'Oh, Mr Bell, if you could just keep him out of the way for ten minutes, that would give us plenty of time.'

'And that only leaves us one problem,' James said. 'We still don't have anywhere to hide Gussie.'

Ernie Bell looked at them. A little smile broke out on his face. 'What's wrong with my back garden?' he said.

'Mr Bell!' said Mandy. 'You're wonderful.'

Ernie Bell shook his head. 'Nothing wonderful about it,' he said. 'You come round to my cottage later and you can tell me the whole story. Just for the minute I'm quite happy to put one over on our Mr High and Mighty temporary postmaster.'

And with that he walked off round the corner of the shed. Pretty soon Mandy and James heard the sound of raised voices.

'Cripes,' said James. 'They must be going at it hammer and tongs if we can hear them from here!'

Mandy grinned. 'That'll certainly keep Mr Barber out of the way,' she said.

James grinned back. 'Right,' he said. 'Let's get that plank off.'

Ernie Bell's walking-stick was perfect for the job. It was made of ash and was very strong. James wedged it into the crack in the planking and put all his weight on it. The wood creaked and groaned under his weight. James leaned harder, his face taut with concentration. Then, at last, there was a loud cracking sound and the plank gave way. So did the one next to it.

'Cripes,' said James, looking at the hole. 'That worked better than I'd bargained for.'

Mandy bent down and hauled the broken planks to one side, leaving a space about thirty centimetres across. There was a hissing and a honking inside the shed, then a bright orange bill appeared in the opening, followed by a creamy head with two bright black eyes. Gussie looked at them suspiciously.

'Come on, Gussie,' Mandy said. 'Please be quiet. Somebody might hear you.'

Gussie stuck her head out farther. Then she honked again.

'She's stuck!' James said.

Mandy bit her lip. There wasn't any time to lose.

Ernie Bell couldn't keep Mr Barber occupied for ever. She bent down to the goose. Gussie was trying to squeeze her way out of the opening.

'Come on Gussie,' Mandy said again. Then she made up her mind. Gussie needed some help – even if she wasn't likely to appreciate it. Mandy got her hands round Gussie's neck and slid them down the feathery body as far as she could.

'Easy does it,' she said, hauling her out.

Gussie looked at her indignantly. Then, with a flurry of feathers, the goose wriggled free and stood flapping her wings. She lowered her neck and hissed.

'Shh!' said Mandy, putting her arms round the goose.

James laughed. 'You sound as bad as Gussie,' he said.

Gussie stopped hissing and honked.

'That's worse than the hissing,' said James. He rummaged in his pocket and took out a piece of string. 'Here. Tie this round her bill.'

'She won't like it,' Mandy said doubtfully.

'She doesn't have to like it,' said James. 'It's for her own good.'

Mandy nodded and tied the string round Gussie's bill.

'Sorry, Gussie,' she said as the goose looked at her accusingly.

James picked Gussie up. Mandy could barely see him behind her. 'Gosh, she's heavy,' he said, staggering a little under the weight. 'I wish we'd remembered the travelling cage.'

'Ouch!' said James as Gussie turned and tapped him smartly on the side of his head with her bill.

'Put your arm round her neck and hold on to her head,' Mandy said.

James lifted his left arm and Gussie promptly unfolded one wing and batted him in the eye.

'Ow!' James yelped, getting his arm round Gussie and pinning her wing to her side.

Gussie shook her head but James clung determinedly to her.

'Watch out you don't hurt her,' Mandy said.

James's flushed face appeared above Gussie's indignant face. 'Me hurt *her*?' he said. 'I'll be black and blue by the time we get to Ernie's place!'

Gussie turned her head slowly and looked James straight in the eye, as if to say 'Just you wait!'

Mandy giggled and James looked offended. 'Honestly,' he said. 'This goose just doesn't appreciate the trouble we're going to for her sake.'

Mandy bit her lip to stop herself giggling again.

'Oh, well,' she said. 'We'll just have to manage.' She peered over Gussie's head at James. 'We've got to get out of here,' she said. 'What's the quickest way to Ernie's house?'

# Seven

Ernie Bell lived in a little cottage a few doors down from Walter Pickard. The row of cottages was behind the Fox and Goose. Ernie's cottage was one of the best-kept cottages in Welford, although it hadn't always been like that. It had been in a terrible state until bossy Mrs Ponsonby decided Ernie was getting too old to look after himself properly and threatened to get him some help. The very next day Ernie had started painting the cottage and ever since he'd kept it neat and sparkling.

'Here we are, Gussie,' said Mandy as they made their way up the back lane that ran behind the cottage gardens.

'Thank goodness for that,' said James. 'You really weigh a ton, Gussie!' he said.

Mandy opened the back gate and James staggered through it with Gussie. He set the goose down on the garden path and blew out his cheeks in relief. Mandy eased off the string round Gussie's bill and gave her a pat on the head. Gussie fluffed up her feathers, spread out her wings and looked at James, completely ignoring Mandy. Then she started to strut towards him. James had turned his back on her. Mandy looked at Gussie. If ever there was a goose determined to get her revenge, this was it!

'Watch out, James!' Mandy cried.

James turned round. Gussie spread her wings, lowered her head and began to hiss. Then she started to run. But James was already running. Round and round the garden they went with Gussie nipping at James's heels. Sammy the squirrel scampered up and down the mesh of his pen, following the chase.

'Call her off!' James yelled as he raced past Mandy for the third time. 'Do something!'

But Mandy was helpless with laughter. 'The tree,' she managed to splutter. 'Geese don't climb trees.'

James veered off, his legs going like pistons, heading straight for the apple tree in the corner of the garden. He was about a metre away when he made a leap for it. Mandy had never seen anybody climb a tree so fast. James scrambled up the tree and sat there on a branch just out of reach of Gussie's long neck. His face was scarlet and his breath was coming in great whoops.

Gussie stood calmly at the bottom of the tree – and waited, hissing a little.

'I'm going to have to spend the night here,' James said miserably. 'Can't you do something?'

Mandy dug in her pocket for some grain, laying a trail of it from the base of the tree across the garden. For a moment Gussie looked as if she was going to ignore it. Then she graciously bent her head and began to nibble at the grain.

Mandy laid the trail over to Sammy's pen. Gussie followed it.

Mandy giggled. 'Oh, look!' she said. 'Look at Sammy. You've got a visitor, Sammy,' Mandy said, going over to the run Ernie had built for the squirrel.

Sammy's little bright eyes darted from Mandy to Gussie. Then he stood up on his hind legs, tiny paws clasped in front of him, and took a good look at the goose. Gussie hissed. Sammy scampered up the wire netting of the run and perched on top of one of the support posts.

'I know just how he feels,' James said mournfully from the apple tree.

'This is Gussie, Sammy,' said Mandy. She turned. 'And this is Sammy, Gussie.'

Gussie's black eyes looked at Sammy. Then she strutted off round the garden, pecking at the grass now and then.

'She looks as if she owns the place,' said James, laughing in spite of himself.

'I think it's safe to come down now, James,' Mandy said.

James shook his head. 'No way,' he said. 'I'm staying put until Ernie gets here.'

'Let's hope he meant what he said about keeping Gussie for the next couple of days,' Mandy said. 'It would be the perfect solution.'

'Oh, I meant it all right,' said a voice behind them. They turned to see Ernie Bell coming through the gate at the back lane. He was carrying a plastic bag and he looked really pleased with himself.

'It's very good of you,' said Mandy. She handed Ernie his walking-stick. 'And thanks for this. It was really useful.'

Ernie took the stick and coughed. 'Nothing to do with being good,' he said gruffly. 'That Mr Barber needs taking down a peg. And don't you worry about anyone else in the village letting on about Gussie being here. I don't think there's anybody left who he hasn't upset.'

'Did you get your parcel back?' James asked.

Ernie looked at him. 'What are you doing up there?' he said. 'It's too early in the year for scrumping apples.'

James grinned and scrambled down from the tree. 'Gussie was after me,' he explained, casting a wary eye at the goose. But Gussie seemed to have forgotten about him.

Ernie threw back his head and laughed. 'Why do you think factories and suchlike keep geese instead of watchdogs?' he said. 'They can be holy terrors.' He took a parcel out of the plastic bag he was carrying. 'I got my parcel back no trouble at all,' he said. 'Bob Davis has a lot more common sense than that Mr Barber.'

Mandy was watching Gussie. 'What about feeding her?' she said.

Ernie dipped into the bag again and brought out a brown paper sack. 'Don't you worry about that,' he said. 'I stopped off to get some grain and there are plenty of vegetables in the garden.'

'You've thought of everything,' James said.

'It's only for two days,' Mandy said. 'And we'll

come round often to see Gussie is all right.'

Ernie Bell looked at Sammy chattering away to Gussie. The goose was standing next to the fence, her head cocked. With her head on one side and her one dark wing she looked comical. At least she seemed to have calmed down.

'It looks as if they're having a good gossip,' Ernie said.

Suddenly Gussie honked and ruffled her feathers.

James looked at his watch. 'Cripes, Mandy,' he said. 'Look at the time. I'll be late for tea. I'd better go.'

'Me too,' said Mandy. 'I want to see how Jack is getting on.' She frowned. 'I still haven't found someone to take him in.' She looked at Ernie Bell. Then she changed her mind. You could only ask so many favours and Ernie was doing enough for them as it was.

She smiled at Ernie. 'We can't thank you enough, Mr Bell. And we'll be round first thing in the morning to see Gussie.'

'Don't you worry about her,' Ernie said. 'I reckon she's made herself at home already.'

Mandy looked round the garden. There was a good sturdy fence all round it. Gussie should be safe enough.

'See you tomorrow, Mr Bell,' Mandy called as she and James left.

But Ernie Bell was looking at Gussie and chuckling to himself. It seemed to Mandy that Ernie was quite pleased with his day's work.

'Got to go! Got to go!' Pippa screeched as Mandy raced into the residential unit.

'She sounds a lot better,' Mandy said, looking at the green and yellow parrot.

Mrs Hope nodded. 'She's making a really good recovery,' she said. 'Soon it *will* be time for her to go.'

Mandy put on a lab coat and began to wash her hands at the sink. 'What about Mr Hapwell's bull?' she said. 'And his cows?'

Mrs Hope shook her head. 'The herd looks as if it's going to be all right,' she said. 'But Dad is a little worried about the bull. It's got a really bad case of ringworm. A fungus can be difficult to get rid of.'

Mandy looked concerned. 'It will be all right, won't it, Mum?' she said.

Mrs Hope smiled. 'Of course it will,' she said. 'But there's a county show next month and Tom Hapwell wants Titan looking his best for that. Ringworm causes big patches of rough skin and loss of hair on the affected area. So it's really unsightly. It isn't serious – just a bit difficult to clear up.'

'That's OK then,' said Mandy. 'Shall I do Jack's dressing?'

Mrs Hope nodded. 'I'll be right there. You're getting really good at dressings,' she said.

Mandy blushed. 'Dad said that the other day,' she said.

'That's because it's true,' said Mrs Hope.

Mandy put on a pair of surgical gloves, took a fresh dressing out of its wrapping and put it into a stainless steel dish.

'Come on, Jack,' she said, taking the little bulldog puppy out of his cage.

Jack looked up at her and yawned. Mandy laughed. 'What a sleepy little thing you are!' she said, scratching the puppy's nose gently.

Jack sneezed.

'Sorry, Jack,' Mandy said. She carried the puppy over to the treatment table and laid him down. He really was the most docile puppy in the world. He wasn't noisy or naughty at all. With his stumpy little legs and tail and his broad brown body he looked like a very small barrel.

'Right,' said Mrs Hope, coming to supervise. 'Let's see how that wound is doing.'

Mandy unwrapped the bandage from around Jack's neck, careful not to disturb the wound.

'He's such a patient animal,' Mrs Hope said as she examined the wound.

'Mr Barber says dogs are dangerous,' Mandy said. 'He should see Jack!'

Jack looked up at her with big brown eyes.

Mrs Hope cleaned the skin round the wound expertly with antiseptic and checked the stitches. 'No infection there,' she said. 'All we have to do is keep it clean and covered until the stitches are ready to come out.'

Mandy took the dressing from the dish and laid it gently over the wound. Then she unwrapped a fresh bandage and began to wind it round the puppy's neck, securing the dressing in place.

'Firmly but not too tightly,' Mrs Hope said.

Mandy concentrated hard. 'There,' she said as she cut the bandage and taped the end in place.

'Good work,' Mrs Hope said approvingly. 'Now you can give him a cuddle.'

Mandy did just that. 'Oh, Jack,' she said. 'I really would like to find somebody local to take you. Then I would be able to see you.'

'No luck yet?' Mrs Hope said.

Mandy shook her head. 'I haven't really had too

much time to do anything about it,' she said. 'I asked Mr Hadcroft but he can't take Jack. Still, he says he'll look out for anyone who can.'

'I'll ask around as well,' Mrs Hope said.

'Thanks, Mum,' Mandy said. 'Jack is such a sweetheart; he'd make anybody a wonderful pet.'

Mrs Hope looked at the puppy consideringly. 'He certainly has a very placid nature,' she said. She wrinkled her forehead. 'You know, Mandy, normally I'd advise finding a home with young, active people in it for a puppy, but Jack is different. It wouldn't have to be a young person. I'm sure he wouldn't be too much of a handful for an older person.'

Mandy thought hard. Who did she know that didn't already have a pet? She sighed. She couldn't think of anybody – except Mr Barber. And she'd rather die than trust Mr Barber with looking after an animal!

'That's the last of the dressings done,' Mrs Hope said. 'Will you clear up while I get tea ready, Mandy?'

Mandy nodded. She loved this time in the residential unit. Just her and the animals. She loved to see them getting better every day. Once she had wiped the work surfaces with disinfectant and tidied the cupboards, she went round and said goodnight to all the animals. Jack was already asleep, curled up and looking like a round brown barrel.

'I'll find somebody to take you, Jack,' Mandy whispered to him. 'I promise I will.'

She was still thinking about Jack later that evening.

'Something on your mind?' Mr Hope said.

Mandy smiled. 'Jack,' she said. 'I just know there must be somebody who'd love to have him as a pet.' She yawned.

'Think about it tomorrow,' Mr Hope said. 'That's the fourth time you've yawned in five minutes.'

'I must be tired,' Mandy said. 'It's all that school work.'

Mr Hope laughed. 'Well, there's no school until Tuesday so you should be able to relax,' he said.

Mandy smiled again. Relax, she thought. She wouldn't be able to relax until Penny and her mum were home and Gussie was truly safe. So long as Mr Barber didn't discover where she was. But Ernie had said nobody in the village would tell him. Mandy yawned again. She hoped Ernie was right.

'Bed,' said Mrs Hope. 'You're asleep on your feet.'

*I've had an exciting day,* Mandy thought but she didn't say so. She wasn't entirely sure what her parents would say about her kidnapping a goose. Goosenapping, she thought as she said goodnight and made her way up the stairs to her bedroom.

She was asleep almost before her head touched the pillow. Gussie was safe and Mandy felt so relieved.

Next day was Saturday. Gran arrived at Animal Ark just before lunch-time.

'You're off then?' Mrs Hope said, putting tea-bags in the pot.

'Off to see where the mood takes you?' Mandy said, teasingly.

Gran nodded at Mandy and smiled. 'Grandad's just gone to fill the camper-van with petrol, then he's picking me up here,' she said. Her eyes twinkled. 'And I've decided on just the spot for lunch. It should take us an hour or so to get there.'

Mrs Hope filled the teapot and set out three bright blue mugs on the pine kitchen table.

'I baked some scones this morning,' Gran said and put a brown paper bag on the table.

'Yum!' said Mandy, opening the bag. 'You're the best baker in the world, Gran.'

Mrs Hope shook her head. 'How did you get the time to do that this morning?' she said to Gran. 'You should give yourself a rest.'

'I'm going to have a rest,' Gran said.

Mrs Hope caught Mandy's eye and winked. 'That'll be the day,' she said.

'I must say though, I'm looking forward to this break,' Gran said as Mandy poured out a cup of tea for her.

'You deserve a break,' Mrs Hope said, sitting down at the table beside Gran. 'You've been doing so much work for the church roof fund.'

'You know Gran,' Mandy said to Mrs Hope. 'If there's a good cause then she's in there doing her best.' She smiled affectionately at her grandmother.

Mrs Hope laughed. 'Too true, Mandy,' she said.

Gran shook her head and smiled. 'Somebody's got to do it,' she said. 'We don't want the roof falling in on Grandad when he's ringing those bells, do we?'

Outside, in the hall, the phone rang.

'I'll get it,' said Mandy. She had the feeling that her mother wanted to give Gran a little lecture about taking it easy.

Mandy held the receiver to her ear.

'Animal Ark. Can I help you?' she said into the mouthpiece.

A voice spluttered on the other end.

'Is that the vet? You've got to do something. There's a goose on the loose in the village and I think it's mine.'

Mandy stared at the receiver. It sounded like Mr Barber.

'Hello! Hello!' the voice spluttered again. 'Is there anybody there? Hello?'

Mandy stood for a moment just staring at the receiver. Mrs Hope came out of the kitchen.

'What is it, Mandy?' she said.

Mandy just looked at her.

'Mandy?' said Mrs Hope.

Mandy thrust the receiver at her mum. 'Got to go, Mum,' she said. 'I'll explain later!'

And she was out of the door and on her bike, racing towards James's house and the village. A goose on the loose. That could mean only one thing: Gussie had escaped!

# Eight

The village was in uproar. Shopkeepers were at the
doors of their shops, people were hanging out of
windows and little Tommy Pickard, Walter's young
grandson, was waddling up the middle of the High
Street flapping his arms. It wasn't difficult to guess
who he was imitating. Mr Hardy from the Fox and
Goose was standing by the door of the pub, doubled
up with laughter.

Mandy and James skidded to a halt beside him.

'Where is she?' Mandy said.

Mr Hardy looked up and wiped tears of laughter
from his eyes.

'Who? Mrs Ponsonby?' he said.

Mandy frowned in puzzlement. 'No,' she said. 'Gussie.'

'You mean the goose?' Mr Hardy said.

Mandy nodded. 'I think it's Gussie, Penny Hapwell's pet goose.'

'One dark wing and a gleam in her eye?' Mr Hardy said, still chuckling.

Mandy nodded.

'That's her all right,' said James.

Mr Hardy shook his head. 'Last I saw of her she was chasing Mrs Ponsonby up Shoemaker Lane,' said Mr Hardy. He started to laugh again. 'Funniest thing I've seen in years.'

'Oh, no,' said James. 'It would have to be Mrs Ponsonby, wouldn't it?'

'Look!' said Mandy, pointing down the road towards the post office.

Mr Barber was standing by the post office door looking at his watch.

'What on earth is he doing?' said James.

Mandy shook her head. 'I don't know,' she said.

Tommy Pickard rushed past, still flapping. 'Mr Barber wants me to catch his goose,' he yelled.

Mandy stuck out a hand and collared him.

'Why doesn't he catch it himself?' Mr Hardy asked.

Tommy grinned. 'He says he can't leave the

post office counter until twelve o'clock exactly,' he said.

Mandy looked at James.

'The post office always closes at twelve o'clock on a Saturday,' James said.

'And Mr Barber is so pernickety, he wouldn't dream of closing a minute before that,' Mandy said.

'So if we can get Gussie before twelve . . .' James began.

Mandy didn't let him finish. Maybe they could make Mr Barber's obsession with rules and regulations work to their advantage.

'Come on,' she said. 'It's nearly twelve now.'

Tommy looked round. 'Where did the goose go?' he said.

There was a screech and a large figure with a flowery hat hanging at an angle on the side of her head came hurtling out of Shoemaker Lane. It was Mrs Ponsonby. She was carrying Pandora, her pudgy Pekinese, under one arm and a small mongrel was dancing and barking round her heels. That was Toby, the little dog Mrs Ponsonby had taken in.

'It's after me!' Mrs Ponsonby shrieked. 'Somebody do something!'

As Mandy and James watched, Toby darted back up Shoemaker Lane and began to bark. There was a hissing sound and Gussie came into view, wings spread, head low.

'There she is!' yelled James.

'Quick!' Mandy shouted. 'We can trap her between us. I'll go this way and you go round by the back road into Shoemaker Lane.'

'Right,' said James and leaped on to his bike.

Mandy propped her own bike against the pub wall and made a dash for Shoemaker Lane.

Mrs Ponsonby came rushing at her. 'Mandy Hope!' she said in a piercing voice. 'Is this anything to do with you?' Then she looked back towards where Shoemaker Lane joined the High Street.

'Can't stop, Mrs Ponsonby,' Mandy called as she rushed past.

'Get that nasty goose away from my Toby,' Mrs Ponsonby screeched after her.

Toby was still circling round Gussie, keeping out of range of her snapping bill. Gussie stretched her neck, lowered her bill and hissed.

'Oh, Gussie,' Mandy cried and ran on. Toby saw her and gave a sharp bark of welcome. Then he was running round her ankles. 'Oh, Toby!' Mandy said, trying not to trip over the little dog.

'I'll get her!' yelled Tommy. He sprinted past Mandy towards Gussie.

Gussie honked and spread her wings even wider, ready to defend herself. Tommy hesitated. He and Gussie looked at each other. Then, quite suddenly, Gussie folded her wings and turned. She had decided to run away rather than stand her ground. But she didn't run back up Shoemaker Lane. She ran down the High Street.

'I'll catch her,' Tommy called back to Mandy. And, brave again, the little boy began to chase Gussie down the High Street.

'No,' Mandy called. 'Not that way, Tommy. You're chasing her in the wrong direction!'

Mandy looked up to see James pedalling furiously down Shoemaker Lane. But it was too late. Tommy had diverted Gussie and she was off, running down the High Street, honking and hissing by turn.

A camper-van braked sharply as Gussie suddenly ran out into the middle of the road. Mandy's heart leaped, but the van stopped in time – just centimetres from the goose. Gussie hissed angrily and flapped on past it. A face looked out of the van window. It was Grandad.

'Catch her, Grandad!' Mandy yelled.

Mandy's grandad looked at her. 'What's going on?' he said.

'It's Gussie, Penny's goose,' Mandy called. 'She's escaped!'

Grandad looked as if he wanted to ask questions but he decided not to. Mandy hurtled past him. Grandad parked the camper-van at the side of the road and ran after Mandy.

'Come back here!' yelled a voice from further up the High Street.

Mandy turned briefly to see who had shouted. James was whizzing down the High Street on his bike. But it was Mr Barber who had shouted. He was standing on the front step of the post office. His face was bright red. He looked ready to burst. Mandy saw him looking at his watch. He wouldn't move from the post office until the dot of twelve. That was something anyway. She glanced quickly at her own watch. Two minutes to go. She had to hurry!

Then she forgot all about Mr Barber as she pounded down the High Street, hot on the trail of Gussie. The goose fluttered and flew and flapped. After her came Tommy and Toby and Mandy and Grandad and James on his bike. At the back, with Pandora under her arm, came Mrs Ponsonby.

In the distance, the church clock began to strike.

Twelve o'clock, Mandy thought. She turned and saw Mr Barber bang the door of the post office behind him and start striding down the High Street. Mandy ran even faster.

James whizzed past on his bike. 'I'll get her!' he yelled back over his shoulder.

Mandy had a stitch in her side. The clock chimes rang out. Even Gussie stopped flapping and fluttering and turned her head towards the sound. In the distance Mandy could see the vicar coming out of the vicarage gate, pushing his bicycle. He mounted his bike and began cycling towards them, his head in the air, not even seeing what was going on. If only he would look. If only he would catch Gussie and whisk her away to safety!

Gussie was in the middle of the road again with Toby at her heels. Mr Hadcroft came freewheeling down the road as if he hadn't a care in the world. But even he couldn't fail to hear the furious barking and honking coming from Toby and Gussie. At last he noticed what was going on. But it was too late. Gussie ran out into his path. The vicar braked too hard. Toby pounced on Gussie. James wobbled and slewed his bike out of the way. There was a series of thumps and crashes and Mandy closed her eyes for a moment.

When she opened them, the vicar and James were sitting in the middle of the road. James had his arm round Gussie's neck and was trying to fend off Toby. The little mongrel clearly thought he had found a new playmate. Mandy panted up with Grandad just behind her. Gussie looked up at her and honked accusingly.

'What on earth is going on?' Grandad said when he got his breath back.

The church clock finished striking twelve and Mrs Ponsonby and Mr Barber arrived together.

Mandy looked at them. It was hard to tell who was going to burst first. They were both out of breath and red faced.

'Toby!' said Mrs Ponsonby. Pandora started barking, trying to struggle out of Mrs Ponsonby's arms. Toby ducked his head and came running to her.

Mrs Ponsonby continued to scold Toby while Mr Barber looked from Mandy to James to Grandad. Tommy Pickard got round behind the vicar, out of the way.

'At least you've caught it,' Mr Barber said grudgingly. Then he looked at Mandy and James suspiciously. 'But what I can't understand,' he went on, 'is how the wretched animal got out in the first place!'

Mandy and James looked at each other. It was clear that Mr Barber hadn't even known Gussie had been missing since last night.

Mr Hadcroft cleared his throat. 'About this goose, Mr Barber,' he said.

Mr Barber looked at him. 'Now, vicar,' he said. 'I hope we aren't going to have any more of that nonsense. This goose is mine.' And he marched over and wrenched Gussie out of James's grasp.

Gussie hissed and tried to nip Mr Barber. But he put his hand firmly round her neck and held her bill away from him.

'Vicious bird,' he said.

'No wonder, the way you treat her,' said Mandy, unable to stop herself. 'Locking her up in a dark shed.'

Mr Barber's eyes narrowed. 'And how do you know where this goose was?' he said. 'Did you have anything to do with this?'

Mandy bit her lip but she didn't get time to reply.

'Mandy is very concerned with animal welfare,' said a loud, authoritative voice and everybody turned to look at Mrs Ponsonby.

Mrs Ponsonby bore down on Mr Barber. Her hat was knocked to one side, her face was bright red and Pandora was squirming under her arm but she looked like a battleship going into action. She planted herself firmly right in front of Mr Barber.

'And if you have been ill-treating any animal I shall personally report you to the RSPCA,' she said. 'We can't have that sort of thing in Welford!'

Mr Barber took a step back. Then he puffed out his chest and looked hard at Mrs Ponsonby.

'More interference!' he said, his face now as red as a beetroot. 'Why don't you all just mind your own business? And especially you!'

And he marched away down the road with Gussie firmly under his arm.

Nobody said anything for a moment. Nobody had ever seen anyone stand up to Mrs Ponsonby.

'Of all the . . .' Mrs Ponsonby started. But she too was speechless.

Grandad stepped forward. 'What's all this about, Mandy?' he said.

Mandy looked at him. It was very tempting to tell him the whole story. But he and Gran were going off on their trip in the camper-van. Gran had a spot all picked out for lunch. She was at Animal Ark at this very moment waiting for Grandad.

If she explained everything to him now, he would put off the trip to help. And what could he do? Mr Barber wouldn't give Gussie back just because

Grandad asked him. If he wasn't frightened of Mrs Ponsonby, he wasn't frightened of anybody.

'I'll tell you when you get back, Grandad,' Mandy said. 'You'd better get going. Gran's waiting for you.'

Grandad looked at his watch. 'So she is,' he said. 'And I promised we'd have a picnic lunch in a favourite spot of hers. If I don't get a move on, we won't be there till teatime.'

Mandy smiled but Grandad still looked concerned.

'There's nothing to worry about, Grandad,' Mandy said. 'It was just a mix-up.'

Grandad frowned. 'I don't believe you,' he said. 'But I suppose it's no good me interfering. You'll tell me about it in your own good time.'

Mandy nodded. It was her problem after all. Only now it all seemed worse than ever.

Mrs Ponsonby wasn't so easily put off. She turned to Mandy. It seemed she had got the power of speech back. Mandy caught Grandad's eye, then she turned to Mrs Ponsonby, bracing herself for a dressing down. After all, Mrs Ponsonby had been chased by a goose and Mandy obviously had something to do with it. It was quite clear that Mrs Ponsonby wanted to know *exactly* what was going on – and who was to blame.

'Let me give you a lift home, Mrs Ponsonby,' Grandad said quickly before she could speak. 'You look all out of puff.'

Mrs Ponsonby gave Mandy a narrow look. For a moment she looked as if she would refuse the lift. But the offer was too good to miss.

'That's very kind of you,' she said.

'Me too?' said Tommy. 'I love your camper-van, Mr Hope.'

Grandad smiled and tousled Tommy's hair. 'You too,' he said.

That left the vicar and Mandy and James.

Mr Hadcroft looked at them. He looked concerned but there was a twinkle in his eye as well.

'Should I ask how Gussie escaped?' he said.

Mandy managed a smile in spite of her problems.

'You'd better not, Mr Hadcroft,' James said.

The vicar nodded. 'I thought not,' he said. He ran a hand through his hair. 'I feel terrible about not being able to do anything about this.'

Mandy shook her head. 'It seems nobody can do anything about Mr Barber,' she said. 'Not even Mrs Ponsonby.'

The vicar nodded his head ruefully. 'You're right there,' he said. 'I reckon Mrs Ponsonby has met her match!'

He got on his bike and cycled off. Mandy watched him. Maybe Mrs Ponsonby had met her match but Mandy Hope hadn't – not by a long shot!

*SPECIAL FOX*

# *Nine*

'What do we do now?' James said, turning to Mandy.

Mandy bit her lip. 'The first thing is to go and see Ernie Bell,' she said. 'We have to find out how Gussie escaped from his garden.'

James frowned. 'I'm sure Ernie was careful,' he said. 'I just hope Mr Barber doesn't know that he helped us to free Gussie.'

Mandy nodded. 'Me too,' she said. 'But I don't think he does. Mr Barber didn't even know Gussie hadn't been in the shed since last night.'

James picked up his bike and started to wheel it along the road. Mandy collected her own bike from beside the Fox and Goose and wheeled it beside him, deep in thought.

'Mr Barber couldn't have been near the shed,' James said. 'If he had, he would have known Gussie wasn't there.'

'Anything could have happened to Gussie,' Mandy said. 'A lot he cares about animals. He left her in that dark place all alone. Goodness knows how long he'll keep her in there now that he's got her back again.'

James coughed and Mandy looked up. She read the thought on James's face. Mr Barber was going to have Gussie for Sunday lunch – with all the trimmings!

'He isn't going to keep her very long, is he?' she said.

James shook his head. 'It seems to me Gussie's days are numbered,' he replied. Behind his glasses his eyes looked serious.

Mandy set her lips in a firm line. 'As far as I'm concerned Gussie's days with Mr Barber are *certainly* numbered,' she said.

James looked at her. 'What do you mean?' he said. 'We've done the best we could.'

Mandy shook her head. 'No, we haven't,' she replied. 'If we'd done the best we could, we'd have been able to save Gussie, wouldn't we? We can do better than that.'

'But what else *can* we do?' said James. 'We've tried kidnapping her and we failed.'

Mandy's head came up and she looked defiantly at James. 'We failed once,' she said.

'So?' said James.

'So we'll have to try again,' said Mandy. 'And this time we won't fail!'

Ernie Bell was in the back garden when they arrived. He turned as they came round the side of the house.

'She's gone,' he said. His old face looked worried.

Mandy and James didn't have to ask who he was talking about.

'We know,' said Mandy.

'She rampaged through the village,' James said.

'She gave Mrs Ponsonby a terrible fright,' Mandy added. 'Gussie chased her all the way down Shoemaker Lane.'

Ernie Bell's eyes lit up for a moment. Ernie and Mrs Ponsonby had never got on too well.

'I would like to have seen that?' he said. Then he saw the expressions on their faces. 'You didn't catch her?' he said.

Mandy shook her head. 'Mr Barber's got her back.'

Ernie Bell took off his cap and scratched his head.

'I should have made the garden more secure,' he said. 'She must have knocked the latch up on the gate.'

Mandy looked round. 'You couldn't have known,' she said. 'Any other goose would have been safe here. It's just that Gussie is quite good at escaping. Penny told us that she sometimes manages to get out of her pen at Twyford. If it's anybody's fault, it's ours.'

Defiantly Ernie put his cap back on his head and drew himself up. 'I'm going down to the post office to make Mr Barber hand that goose over,' he said.

Mandy laid a hand on his arm. 'It's no good,' she said. 'Mr Hadcroft has tried, we've tried, Mrs Ponsonby has tried. Mr Barber says he won Gussie fair and square. She belongs to him.' She shook her head.

Mandy felt as if there was no point in even trying again. But Ernie Bell was looking at her.

'You aren't going to give up, are you?' he said.

'Mandy?' said James. 'Give up? When does Mandy Hope ever give up when there's an animal in trouble?'

And suddenly Mandy felt her depression seep away. What had Gran said? 'Somebody's got to do it.' The Hopes didn't give up. James was right. She wasn't a Hope for nothing.

'Of course we aren't going to give up,' she said. 'We're going to get Gussie back again!'

Ernie Bell was smiling now. 'Good for you,' he said. Then he became brisk and businesslike. 'What are you going to do? Can I help?'

Mandy smiled back at him. She felt heaps better. 'If James and I get Gussie back, can we bring her to you again?' she asked.

Ernie Bell looked pleased. 'I'm glad you'd trust me with her again,' he said.

Mandy smiled. 'Of course we would,' she said. 'Wouldn't we, James?'

James beamed. 'Sure thing,' he said to Ernie. 'After all, you were part of the rescue team, Mr Bell.'

Ernie held out his stick. 'If he locks her in that shed again you'll need this,' he said. 'Now you two get going. I've got work to do.'

James took the stick. 'Thanks,' he said.

'What work?' said Mandy, puzzled.

Ernie winked at them. 'You get that goose and bring her back here,' he said. 'And I'll make sure she doesn't get out again.'

'What are you going to do?' said Mandy.

'Do?' said Ernie. I'm going to make this garden

gooseproof. That's what I'm going to do,' he said.

The last thing Mandy and James saw as they wheeled their bikes out into the lane was Ernie Bell collecting his box of tools.

James laughed as they pedalled away from Ernie's cottage. 'By the time he's finished, nothing will be able to get in or out of that garden,' he said.

'Mmm,' said Mandy.

James looked at her. 'What are you thinking?' he said.

Mandy frowned. 'I was wondering when it would be safe to go for Gussie,' she said.

James thought. 'Tomorrow's Sunday,' he said.

Mandy nodded. 'We can't wait until tomorrow,' she said. 'It's too risky. We have to try today.'

James shook his head. 'But when?' he said.

Mandy pursed her lips. 'Tonight. After dark,' she said.

James drew in his breath. 'You mean sneak out?' he said.

Mandy turned to him. 'It's the only way, James,' she said. 'You know what will happen to Gussie if we don't do anything. This is an emergency!'

James looked worried. 'I've never sneaked out of the house in the middle of the night before,' he said. 'Mum and Dad would be furious with me.'

'We *have* to, James,' Mandy insisted. 'Don't you see? It's the only chance we have of saving Gussie. Think of Penny.'

Mandy waited, biting her lip, while James thought about it.

'OK,' he said at last. 'We'll do it. When?'

Mandy breathed a sigh of relief. 'It has to be after the whole village is asleep,' she said. 'What about midnight? We should be safe by then.'

James took a deep breath. 'OK. Midnight,' he said as they headed their bikes back towards Animal Ark.

'I'll meet you at the end of the road,' Mandy said.

'How are you going to get out?' said James.

Mandy shrugged. 'The same way as you,' she said. 'Quietly!'

# *Ten*

Mandy looked at the illuminated face of her bedside clock. It was almost midnight. She had nearly dropped off to sleep once or twice but each time she had jerked awake. There was no time for sleeping when there was an animal to be saved.

Mandy had laid out a black jumper and her darkest jeans, ready to slip on. She pulled the jumper over her head and slid into her jeans. She picked up her trainers and the torch she had hidden under her bed. It was better to wait until she got downstairs before putting her shoes on.

She crept in stockinged feet down the stairs from her bedroom, stopping every time there was the slightest creak. That was the trouble with old houses, everything creaked. Especially the stairs. But when you lived in an old house you got so used to the creaks you hardly heard them. So maybe her parents wouldn't hear anything after all.

At last she was downstairs. She put on her trainers, lifted the latch of the door gently and was off into the night.

Shadows shifted as thin cloud passed across the face of the moon. Somewhere an owl hooted. Mandy crept down the path towards the road, careful to make no sound.

Moonlight silvered the hedgerows and a small breeze stirred the grass verges. Mandy strained her eyes towards the road end. The hedge made a deep shadow on the road. Something moved against the hedge and a figure stepped forward. For a moment Mandy's breath caught in her throat. The figure had a hook-shaped horn sticking out of its head. She looked up in alarm.

'It's only me,' said a voice.

Mandy's breath came out in a rush. It was James. 'Hi!' he said softly.

'What's that?' said Mandy.

James looked puzzled, then he reached a hand back and touched the hook.

'It's Ernie's stick,' he said. 'I shoved it down the back of my anorak.'

Mandy laughed with relief. 'You gave me a fright,' she said. 'I thought you were a monster.'

James grinned. 'You got away all right?' he said.

Mandy nodded. Then her heart lurched again as a really black shadow moved towards her. Something warm and furry brushed against her hand.

'Blackie!' she said on a gasp. She looked at James. 'What do you want to do?' she said. 'Scare me to death?'

James's teeth showed white for a moment in the moonlight. 'Sorry about that,' he said. 'Either I had to bring him or he would have woken the whole house.'

'Just so long as he keeps quiet,' Mandy said as they set out for the post office.

They walked on, the moonlight bright enough for them to see the road ahead.

'There it is,' said Mandy as the post office came into view.

They made their way round the side. Blackie padded silently beside them. He was usually the most disobedient dog on earth but tonight he seemed to realise how important it was to keep beside them and not to make a noise. The shed loomed up in front of them. It seemed bigger in the moon-light.

'I suppose he has put Gussie back in that shed,' James said.

Mandy nodded. 'Where else would he put her?' she said. 'He could hardly keep a goose in his flat.'

'I bet he's nailed those planks back on,' James said. 'It won't be too easy to get them off this time.'

Mandy opened her mouth to reply but she was cut short. Suddenly the silence was broken by an unearthly sound. The noise shattered the stillness of the night. It sounded a bit like a foghorn, only sharper. And it didn't stop. It went on and on, getting louder all the time.

'What's that?' James said.

Mandy froze and even Blackie shrank against her, his tail between his legs.

Mandy looked down at the terrified Labrador. 'There's only one way to find out,' she said. 'Come on.'

Then she was off, her long legs covering the ground.

'Wait for me,' James yelled, pelting after her.

Mandy was round the corner and standing beside the shed. James came running up.

'It's Gussie,' Mandy said.

'But why is she making that awful racket?' said James.

Mandy's face froze.

'Mandy!' said James.

But Mandy didn't answer. She was watching Blackie. Blackie was nosing around the bottom of the shed door. He looked up and whined. Then he gave a howl and the whites of his eyes showed.

James jumped and looked at the Labrador. 'What on earth's got into him?' he said. Then he turned to Mandy. 'Mandy?' he said again. 'What is it?'

Mandy pointed to the door of the shed. She switched on her torch. Thin wisps of smoke were coming out from under the door.

'The shed,' said Mandy. 'It's on fire! That's why Blackie howled. And that's why Gussie is honking like that. She's terrified.'

'She's trapped in there,' James said. 'The shed's on fire and she's locked in!'

'Quick!' Mandy said to James. 'The stick!'

James tried to wedge the stick behind the broken planks.

'It won't fit,' he said. 'Mr Barber has nailed the planks down too tightly.'

'Let me try,' said Mandy and grabbed the stick from him. She tried to wedge the stick under the planks but she couldn't get it behind them.

'I told you,' said James.

Mandy turned a desperate face to James. Inside the shed, Gussie was hissing and flapping. Mandy's heart went out to the poor creature, locked in there.

'She must be terrified,' Mandy said. 'Look! There's more smoke now.'

'I'll go for help,' James said.

Mandy looked up towards the rooms above the post office. Everything was in darkness.

'You'd better see if you can wake up Mr Barber first,' she said.

James nodded. 'I'll try,' he said. 'I'll be back as soon as I can.'

Mandy watched as James ran off towards the front of the post office. She bit her lip. Smoke was beginning to pour under the door now. She flung herself at the door. Although it was padlocked, she felt it move slightly. She kicked the door in frustration.

Suddenly a light went on in the flat above her and she saw the padlock clearly. It was new and solid looking. There was no way she could force it.

A window shot up and a head leaned out.

'What's all that noise?' shouted a voice. It was Mr Barber.

Mandy looked up. Mr Barber was hanging out of an upstairs window.

'It's the shed!' Mandy shouted. 'You've got to come down and unlock it.'

'Who is that?' Mr Barber shouted back. 'What are you doing down there?' His hair was tousled and his face was red with anger.

'It's me!' yelled Mandy. 'Mandy Hope. Please, Mr Barber. You've got to come down and let Gussie out.'

Mr Barber's voice rose even more. 'It's you, is it?' he yelled. 'We'll see about this, young woman. Coming here disturbing people in the middle of the night. Do you know what time it is?'

'But the shed's on fire!' Mandy shouted.

Her voice was drowned out by Mr Barber. He was still yelling at her.

'Young vandals! I'm phoning your parents – and the police,' he bellowed. He slammed the window shut and there was silence for a moment.

Then Mandy heard a furious hammering from the front of the post office and James's voice raised urgently. Blackie began barking.

Mandy looked in desperation at the door. It would take James time to explain to Mr Barber. He wasn't the type of person to take much notice of what people said to him – especially not James or Mandy. He obviously thought they were up to no good.

Mandy could hear Gussie getting more and more panicky. She couldn't wait any longer. Gussie might be overcome by the smoke any minute, even though the shed was quite big. It stood about three metres high but smoke filled a space very quickly. There had to be something she could do.

Mandy felt the weight of Ernie Bell's stick in her hand. It was a good heavy one. She looked again at the shed door. The padlock might be sturdy but the door wasn't. It was a very old shed and the wood was rotten in some places. If she couldn't force the padlock, maybe she could loosen it from its moorings.

She took a deep breath, raised the stick and brought it crashing down on the padlock. The padlock rattled but didn't give way. Mandy turned the stick round. She raised it again and hit the padlock with the handle. Still the padlock held. There were tears in her eyes now. She raised the stick once more and crashed it down on the padlock with all her strength.

There was a splintering sound and part of the door jamb that held the padlock gave way. The padlock hung useless as the door swung open. At once there

was a flurry of wings and feathers and Gussie flapped, screeching out into the night.

Mandy dropped Ernie's stick and flung herself on Gussie, gathering the goose up into her arms. Gussie flapped and fussed, stretching her neck, trying to get away from Mandy. Mandy held her tightly. She didn't want Gussie rushing around in the dark, maybe injuring herself.

'Oh, Gussie, Gussie, you're safe!' she cried.

She looked into the shed. Flames were flickering at the back. As she watched, a pile of papers suddenly caught fire and the flames grew. Then the back of the shed caught light and Mandy gasped in horror. The shed backed directly on to the post office. If something wasn't done soon, the whole post office would catch fire!

James ran round the corner of the shed. 'He's coming down,' he gasped. 'Finally!'

Mandy pointed at the leaping flames. 'Get him to phone the fire-brigade, James,' she said. 'I'll run to the Fox and Goose and get Mr Hardy.'

A figure lurched round the corner. 'What's all this?' said Mr Barber. He was wearing a checked dressing-gown over his pyjamas. He looked really angry when he saw Mandy. Then his eyes went to the shed. 'Young vandals!' he yelled. 'Arsonists!'

Mandy set Gussie down on the ground. The goose seemed calmer now. 'It wasn't us,' she cried. 'Please, Mr Barber, you've got to ring the fire-brigade. James and I are going for help.'

And, without waiting to hear what he said, Mandy and James ran for the Fox and Goose.

It took a while to rouse Mr Hardy but, as soon as he saw who was hammering on the door of the pub, he came down at once.

'Fire?' he said and he looked down the High Street.

'The shed backs right on to the post office,' James said. 'If the fire spreads, the whole place could go up in flames.

'And not only the post office. The whole village could be at risk,' Mr Hardy said. He looked up at the sky. Then he licked a finger and held it up, testing the direction of the breeze. 'Let's just hope this breeze doesn't turn into a wind.'

'What can we do?' Mandy said to Mr Hardy. 'We might not have much time if the fire really takes hold. And the fire-brigade has to come all the way from Walton.'

The three kilometres to Walton had never seemed so far.

Mr Hardy ran for the phone. 'I'll phone the fire-brigade,' he said. 'Mandy, you get round as many houses as you can. We'll need buckets and hoses if possible. James, you run to the church and get Mr Hadcroft to start ringing the church bells.'

'What?' said James.

'Just do it. Now!' Mr Hardy said and disappeared into the pub.

'The church bells?' James said to Mandy.

Mandy gave him a push. 'It'll wake the village,' she said. 'Go, James! Hurry!'

James sped off towards the church and Mandy raced along the High Street, knocking on doors, explaining breathlessly. Then the sound of the church bells rang out across the village. The bells pealed their message of danger, wakening Welford, calling the villagers from their beds. Mandy stood listening in the High Street. Already lights were going on all over Welford. If everyone turned out then surely they could save the village.

# Eleven

'Keep them going!' Mr Hardy shouted.

Mandy's arms were aching. She passed the bucket from one hand to the other, trying to keep the water from sloshing over. She cast a quick glance across the road to the village hall. She could see her father directing operations as he and Ernie Bell filled bucket after bucket from the standpipe outside the hall, passing them down the line. He and Mrs Hope had been among the first to arrive. Mandy had felt awful when she had seen how worried they were.

'Your bed was empty,' Mrs Hope said.

Mandy bit her lip. 'I'll explain later, Mum,' she said.

Mr Hope had looked very serious indeed. 'The explanation had better be good, young lady,' he said and Mandy's heart sank.

'As long as you're OK,' Mrs Hope said and gave Mandy a quick hug before they both rushed off to help with the fire-fighting.

But Mandy knew she wouldn't get off easily. She had a lot of explaining to do. For the moment, though, she concentrated on passing the buckets up the line to Mr Hardy and Walter Pickard. There were plenty of helpers now. It seemed as if the whole village was there. They had formed a human chain, passing buckets of water from hand to hand. Mr Hardy and Walter were at the front of the line, throwing the water on the fire. But all they were doing was keeping the fire from spreading. The shed at the back was ablaze now. There was nothing they could do about that. But they could try to save the post office and the rest of the village.

Mandy looked towards the post office. Mr Hardy had broken down the front door and, sure enough, the fire had spread from the shed behind and reached the back of the shop. She could see the glow of flames from inside.

'There's government property in there,' Mr Barber was shouting. 'And I'm responsible for it.'

Mandy looked at him. He was working harder than anybody, swinging the heavy buckets from hand to hand, never stopping even for a moment. His dressing-gown was covered with dirt and his face was filthy. He looked down at Mandy.

'Tired?' he asked.

Mandy was almost too surprised to answer. She nodded.

'You're doing a good job,' he said. 'Keep it up. The fire-brigade shouldn't be long now. It's only three kilometres from Walton to Welford.'

There was a wailing sound far in the distance along the Walton road and Mandy looked round with relief.

'The fire-brigade,' she shouted. 'They're coming!'

But Mr Hardy didn't stop for a moment. 'Keep going,' he shouted down the line. 'We're barely managing to keep that fire at bay.'

Mandy looked towards the post office. Mr Hardy was right. There were more flames now. As she watched, flames leaped up and licked at a shelf of magazines and comics. She watched, horrified, as they began to smoke, the paper curling. Then the whole shelf burst into flames and comics and magazines came cascading down on to the floor of the shop, knocking over a display of breakfast cereal.

One of the boxes burst, spilling cereal all over the floor.

Mr Barber rushed forward with a bucket and ran into the shop, throwing the water over the burning paper.

'Get out of there!' Mr Hardy shouted.

Mr Barber looked up, his face lit by the flames. The wailing of the fire-engine was getting louder. Mr Barber stumbled out of the shop, knocking over a rack of vegetables. Then the wailing of the siren was cut off and the fire-engine screeched to a halt in front of the post office.

Firemen leaped down from the vehicle, running for the water main, attaching a hose.

'Stand back!' said a fireman in a white helmet. 'We'll deal with this.'

Mr Hardy looked at Mandy. 'Now I know how they felt in the Wild West when the cavalry arrived,' he said. Then he scratched his chin. 'I must get a photo of Gussie,' he said.

Mandy looked at him, puzzled. Then she remembered. 'You mean to go with Lucky's picture?'

Lucky was a little fox cub Mandy and James had rescued. Mr Hardy had his photograph up over the bar in the Fox and Goose.

Mr Hardy nodded. 'I've got the fox,' he said. 'And

I reckon Gussie would make the perfect goose.' He grinned. 'And just think of the stories I'd be able to tell the customers about them.'

Mandy couldn't help smiling. Trust Mr Hardy to cheer her up! She began to cross the road to the village hall. Then her smile disappeared as she saw her dad walking towards her. It seemed the time for explanations had come.

'Uh-oh,' said James, coming to stand beside her. 'This looks like trouble.'

Mr Hope stopped in front of them and looked at Mandy.

'Have you any idea how worried your mother and I were when we found your bed empty?' he said. 'What's going on? Where were you?'

Mandy's heart sank. When her dad said 'your mother and I' in that tone of voice it meant trouble.

'It was Gussie,' she said. 'Mr Barber was going to eat Gussie for Sunday lunch. He had her locked up in the shed at the back of the post office. We had to rescue her.'

'We?' said Mr Hope ominously.

James shuffled uncomfortably. 'It wasn't only Mandy. It was me as well. We couldn't just abandon Gussie,' he said.

'I might have known there would be some kind of

animal at the root of this,' Mr Hope said, running his hand through his hair.

Mandy held her breath. Was she going to be grounded for a month? Then Mr Hope shook his head.

'Mr Barber was really going to have Gussie for lunch?' he said.

Mandy and James nodded and Mr Hope gave a sigh. 'Kids!' he exclaimed. He looked at James. 'Your dad is on the warpath,' he said.

James went pale and Mr Hope smiled. 'You two deserve to be grounded for a year,' he said. 'But I suppose I'll go and have a word with your dad, James.'

'Thanks, Mr Hope,' James said with relief.

'But don't think you're going to get away with this kind of thing,' he said. 'Your dad and I will think up some kind of punishment for the two of you.'

'That could have been worse,' James said, after Mr Hope had walked away.

Mandy sagged with relief. Her arms felt as if they were coming out of their sockets. She looked at James. His face was streaked with sweat and smoke and his glasses were sitting halfway down his nose.

Mandy smiled at him ruefully. 'We don't know the

worst yet,' she said. 'I wonder what the punishment will be?'

'Thank goodness the fire-brigade has arrived,' James said. 'I couldn't have kept that up much longer.'

Mandy nodded. The firemen were round the back of the post office, dealing with the blazing shed. Mandy frowned and looked round.

'Where's Gussie?' she said.

James shook his head. 'I don't know,' he said.

Mandy looked round again. Almost the whole village had turned out by now. They were milling around, talking to each other, trying to find out exactly how the fire had started. But there was no goose amongst them. Gussie had disappeared.

'She was here a moment ago,' said James.

Then the breath caught in Mandy's throat. There, inside the post office, was Gussie. Mandy looked at the floor of the shop. It was covered in breakfast cereal and vegetables. Some boxes had fallen down and the poor goose was trapped behind them. A piece of burning paper floated from the shop counter and Gussie began to hiss, flapping her wings, terrified.

'What on earth is she doing in there?' James said, following Mandy's eyes.

'Look at the floor,' Mandy said. 'Gussie must have been hungry. She must have been attracted by the cereal and vegetables.'

'And now she's trapped,' said James.

Mandy shoved her hair back with a dirty hand. 'I've got to get her out,' she said.

'You can't go in there,' said James. 'It's dangerous. The fire-brigade will get her once they've got the fire in the shed under control.'

'That might be too late,' Mandy said.

Another box fell from a shelf and started burning.

'You can't do it, Mandy,' James said.

Mandy turned to him. Her smoke-blackened face was streaked with tears. 'We can't just leave her,' she said. 'I'm going in.'

And she took a step forward.

'Oh, no you don't,' said a voice and Mr Barber stepped in front of her.

Mandy looked at him in despair. Not again. As if Mr Barber hadn't caused them enough trouble!

'How can you be so cruel?' she said to him bitterly. 'Don't you realise that Gussie would have woken you – even if we hadn't been there? Don't you understand that you could have been trapped upstairs if that fire had taken hold? It was Gussie that raised the alarm. And now you're just going to let her die in there!'

Mr Barber looked at her. His round pink face was streaked with dirt and his dressing-gown was wet and filthy. The pernickety Mr Barber was looking dirty and untidy – he must be furious.

'I know that,' he said. 'I know I could have been trapped upstairs if it hadn't been for you two – and Gussie.'

Mandy looked at him, her eyes wide with surprise. He had said 'Gussie' – not 'that goose' or 'that animal'. Mandy was speechless.

But Mr Barber was speaking again. 'That's why you aren't going in there,' he said. '*I* am.'

And before Mandy could draw breath, Mr Barber had made a dash for the post office.

# Twelve

'Cripes!' said James. 'Do you think he'll make it?'

'What's going on over there?' Mr Hardy shouted from the steps of the village hall. Then he and all the others were crossing the street, staring at the post office.

Mandy bit her lip. Mr Barber was in the doorway of the post office.

'Gussie's trapped in there,' she said. 'Mr Barber's gone to rescue her.'

The crowd moved to join them. Every head was turned towards the post office and the figure of Mr Barber. Mandy saw him making his way towards Gussie. He stumbled and almost fell, choking on the smoke. Mandy held her breath. Papers and boxes were catching light, falling in front of him, blocking his path. Then she saw Mr Barber make a dive, his arms outstretched. There was a furious honking and hissing and Mr Barber turned towards them again with Gussie in his arms.

The whole crowd let out a cheer as fat little Mr Barber made a dash for the door. A burning carton fell right in front of him.

'Jump!' yelled Mandy. And, to her surprise, Mr Barber did just that.

He leaped over the box and through the door, Gussie clutched tightly in his arms. Then he was

surrounded by people, clapping him on the back, saying what a brave person he was.

Mandy looked at him standing there with Gussie in his arms. He looked back at her.

'She's yours,' he said. 'And I don't want another one to replace her.' He smiled and suddenly he looked really friendly. 'I'll never eat goose again!' he said.

'You mean it?' Mandy said. 'You're really going to give Gussie back?'

Mr Barber held Gussie out to her.

'I mean it,' he said. 'If it hadn't been for you two, I would have been trapped upstairs.'

James interrupted. 'We came to steal Gussie again,' he said.

Mr Barber raised his eyebrows. 'Again?' he said.

Mandy and James looked at each other. 'That's how she got out of the shed the first time,' Mandy explained. 'We took her. We couldn't let you eat Penny's pet.'

Mr Barber looked seriously at them and for a moment Mandy thought he was going to start giving them a row again.

Instead, he shook his head from side to side as if trying to come to terms with something.

'Animals really are important to you, aren't they?' he said.

Mandy smiled. 'Of course they are,' she said. 'More important than anything.' She paused. 'We *need* animals,' she said.

Mr Barber smiled back. 'I'm beginning to understand that now. And I've been a fool,' he said. 'You were right about that German Shepherd too.'

'Sheba,' Mandy said.

Mr Barber nodded. 'Sheba,' he said. 'I thought it was just a lot of nonsense – that business of her coming to get help. But it isn't nonsense, is it?'

Mandy shook her head. 'Animals are our friends,' she said. 'We should care about them.'

'You've taught me that,' Mr Barber said. 'You cared enough about Gussie to steal her – twice!'

James looked uncomfortable. 'It wasn't exactly stealing,' he said. 'More like rescuing.'

Mr Barber nodded. 'Still,' he said, 'it couldn't have been easy. You must have been scared. I mean, I know I'm not very good at getting on with people.'

Mandy let out a laugh. 'We were terrified,' she said.

There was a flurry of activity and a fireman bustled up to them. It was the one with the white helmet – the one in charge. He was holding something in his hands.

'We found this in the shed at the back,' he said. 'We think it might have started the fire.'

Mr Barber looked at what the fireman was holding.

'It's my pipe,' he said. 'I must have dropped it in the shed earlier when I was putting some food out for Gussie.'

'Gussie?' said the fireman looking puzzled.

'This goose,' said Mr Barber, pointing at Gussie who was scratching around his feet.

'Oh, the goose,' said the fireman. 'I've just been hearing about that. It seems the goose gave the alarm. You're a lucky chap. That pipe could have smouldered for hours.' He shook his head and looked very seriously at Mr Barber. 'Everybody makes mistakes, sir,' he said. 'And I'm sure it was an accident you dropping that smouldering pipe. But if it hadn't been for this goose, things could have been a lot different.'

Mr Barber hung his head. 'I know that,' he said. He pointed at Mandy and James. 'These two had a hand in the thing as well.'

The fireman grinned at Mandy and James. 'So I understand,' he said. 'And we won't ask what they were doing out of bed at this time of night.'

Mandy and James shuffled uncomfortably.

'Ah well,' said the officer to Mr Barber. 'As I said, everybody makes mistakes.'

Ernie Bell wandered up in time to hear that. He chuckled. 'Hear that, Mr Barber?' he said. 'Everybody makes mistakes – even you.'

Mr Barber turned to Ernie as the fireman walked back to his fire-engine.

'Dropping that pipe was only one of my mistakes,' he said. He hesitated. 'I'm sorry if I was difficult about that parcel – and all the other things. I just wanted to do things right.' He looked suddenly quite old somehow. 'I don't usually get out much,' he said. 'And I don't have any friends. Since I retired I guess I've been a bit of a loner really.'

Ernie looked at him. 'Ah well,' he said. 'It looks as if you've learned your lesson now.' And he wandered off. Then he turned back, as if remembering something. 'If you want to try your hand at a bit of bell-ringing,' he said, 'we could always do with a bit of help.'

Mr Barber looked surprised and pleased. 'I'd like that,' he said. 'I'd like that very much.'

Ernie nodded. 'Wednesday evening at the church,' he said. 'See you there.'

Mandy put a hand on Mr Barber's dirty sleeve.

'Did you really mean what you said about changing

your mind about animals?' she said.

Mr Barber looked at her. 'Every word,' he said.

Mandy smiled. 'You know, if you're lonely, having a pet is a good idea.'

'You could get a dog,' said James. 'Dogs are great fun.'

'After what I said about them?' Mr Barber said.

'But you've changed your mind,' Mandy said.

Mr Barber looked wistful. 'Do you think a dog would be a good idea?' he said. 'I've never been very fond of dogs.'

Mandy took a deep breath. 'That's because you're afraid of them,' she said. 'It's sensible to be careful of strange dogs. But you're scared of *all* dogs – even Blackie.'

Mr Barber looked as if he was going to deny it. Then he said, 'You know, I think you might be right.'

Mandy smiled. She knew she was right. And she knew the *perfect* puppy for Mr Barber.

# Thirteen

'Oh, thank you, Mandy!' said Penny, bending down and cuddling Gussie. 'And you too, James,' she added.

Mandy smiled at Penny. It was Monday afternoon. Mandy and James had taken Gussie to be photographed by Mr Hardy. Now they were back at Twyford Farm.

'She wasn't any trouble, was she?' Penny said anxiously, standing up.

Mandy and James looked at each other. They had agreed that they wouldn't mention Gussie's adventures to Penny. The thought of her pet being locked in Mr Barber's shed – and almost being killed in a fire – would be too upsetting for her.

Gussie waddled over and fluffed up her feathers, leaning close to Mandy. Mandy looked down at her. She seemed none the worse for her ordeal.

'Gussie was no trouble at all,' Mandy said.

Penny beamed at them. 'I just knew she'd be safe with you,' the little girl said.

James coughed and went a bit red and Mandy bit her lip as she remembered what a narrow escape Gussie had had. But they were saved from replying as Mr Hope and Tom Hapwell came out of the cattle shed.

'Those pellets in the feed worked wonders with the herd,' Tom said.

'We caught it in time,' Mr Hope said. 'And I'm pleased about Titan. He's making really good progress.'

Mr Hapwell shook his head. 'Ringworm!' he said. 'Ah well, it's clearing up now. He should be fine for the county show next month.'

'He'll be completely recovered by then,' Mr Hope said. 'Just keep him isolated for a while longer.' He turned to Mandy and James. 'We'd better get going,' he said. 'We've got another call to make.'

Mandy and James grinned at him. They certainly had! Jack was tucked up in the back of the Land-rover, waiting for them. Mrs Hope had taken the stitches out that morning and Jack was as fit as a fiddle.

'Come on, you two,' Mr Hope said. 'I've got something to say to the pair of you.'

Mandy and James jumped into the Land-rover and waved goodbye to Penny and her dad – and Gussie.

'Now,' said Mr Hope as they drove away from Twyford. 'About this punishment of yours.'

Mandy and James glanced at each other. What would it be?

'I want the two of you to do at least an hour every day at Animal Ark, cleaning cages, exercising puppies, being helpful instead of getting into scrapes,' Mr Hope said.

Mandy let out a great whoosh of laughter. 'But, Dad, that isn't a punishment,' she said. 'Helping at Animal Ark is a pleasure, isn't it, James?'

James nodded enthusiastically and his glasses nearly jumped off his nose.

'In that case we'll make it only half an hour,' Mr Hope joked. 'Oh, and there's one more thing.'

'What's that?' Mandy said warily.

'You've got to drop by and give Gran all the news,' Mr Hope said. 'She and Grandad got back this morning and Gran says she's missed all the excitement.'

'We'll go round there this afternoon,' Mandy said.

'After we've been to the post office,' James said.

'Oh, yes,' said Mandy. 'After that.' She turned and looked at Jack, asleep on a rug in the back of the Land-rover. 'I've found you a new home, Jack,' she said. 'I'm sure I have.'

'It doesn't look too bad,' James said as Mr Hope dropped them off in front of the post office.

Mandy nodded. 'The shed is destroyed,' she said. 'But it was ready to be knocked down anyway.'

They stood for a moment in front of the post office. Ernie Bell had fixed the door where Mr Hardy had had to break it down and it looked as good as new.

'OK,' said Mandy, cuddling Jack. 'I'm ready.'

The puppy looked up at her with melting brown eyes. How could anyone not fall in love with him?

James opened the post office door and Mandy walked through it with Jack in her arms. There was still a faint smell of charred timbers but the damage really wasn't too bad and the shop was as tidy and neat as always. Mr Barber looked up from behind the counter. He must have worked very hard to get it back into order.

'Business as usual,' he said and smiled at them.

Then his eyes went to Jack. 'Who's this?'

Mandy took a deep breath. 'This is Jack, Mr Barber,' she said. 'He's just a puppy and he needs a home.' She hesitated. 'I thought perhaps you might want him,' she finished.

Mr Barber looked at her for a moment, then he came round the side of the counter and stood in front of her.

'Me?' he said.

Mandy nodded. 'I think it would be such a good idea,' she said. 'What you need is a puppy. You couldn't possibly be afraid of a puppy. And once you've trained him and looked after him, you won't be afraid of other dogs either.'

Mr Barber looked doubtful. 'I'm not as young as I was,' he said. 'Puppies have a lot of energy.'

Mandy smiled. 'Not Jack,' she said. 'He's such a contented little thing. He has a wonderful nature.'

Mr Barber came closer and looked carefully at Jack. 'He's a bulldog puppy,' he said, smiling.

'Hold him,' said Mandy.

Mr Barber reached out and took Jack from her, cradling him in his arms. The little puppy put his head on one side, and looked at Mr Barber. Then he scrambled up, placed his two front paws on Mr Barber's shoulders and licked his face.

'He likes me,' said Mr Barber.

'Of course he does,' said Mandy, looking from tubby little Mr Barber to tubby little Jack. 'You were made for each other,' she said.

She and James exchanged a look and Mandy smiled. With a little bit of help, Mr Barber and Jack were going to be just fine.